Down below, she caught a flash of movement. Her attackers were catching up.

"Where are you taking me?"

"Some place safe where we can call for help. Trust me, I know this part of the forest."

What choice did she have? She'd prayed for God to send help and He had. Of all the people in the world, He'd sent Bryan.

"Come on." He held his hand out to her. The August sun beat down on them, the air thick with heat. Down below, the two thugs were weaving their way up the mountain.

"Where are we going anyway?"

"We need to get help, call the sheriff," he said.

She stared up at the rocky terrain. "Isn't there an easier way?"

"Sarah, would you trust me? I know where I'm going. Those guys won't be able to follow us. They'll give up."

It was the first time he'd said her name. The warmth in his voice only reminded her of ten-year-old wounds. "I really don't have a choice here. I'll do what you say." She wasn't so sure about the men giving up, though.

Books by Sharon Dunn

Love Inspired Suspense

Dead Ringer
Night Prey
Her Guardian
Broken Trust
Zero Visibility
Guard Duty
Montana Standoff

SHARON DUNN

has always loved writing, but didn't decide to write for publication until she was expecting her first baby. Pregnancy makes you do crazy things. Three kids, many articles and two mystery series later, she still hasn't found her sanity. Her books have won awards, including a Book of the Year award from American Christian Fiction Writers. She was also a finalist for an *RT Book Reviews* Inspirational Book of the Year award.

Sharon has performed in theater and church productions, has degrees in film production and history, and worked for many years as a college tutor and instructor. Despite the fact that her résumé looks as if she couldn't decide what she wanted to be when she grew up, all the education and experience have played a part in helping her write good stories.

When she isn't writing or taking her kids to activities, she reads, plays board games and contemplates organizing her closet. In addition to her three kids, Sharon lives with her husband of twenty-two years, three cats and lots of dust bunnies. You can reach Sharon through her website, www.sharondunnbooks.net.

MONTANA STANDOFF

SHARON DUNN

HARLEQUIN® LOVE INSPIRED® SUSPENSE

Recycling programs
for this product may
not exist in your area.

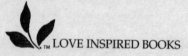

™ LOVE INSPIRED BOOKS

ISBN-13: 978-0-373-44561-5

MONTANA STANDOFF

www.Harlequin.com

Printed in U.S.A.

For you know that it was not with the perishable things such as silver or gold that you were redeemed from the empty way of life handed down to you from your ancestors, but with the precious blood of Christ, a lamb without blemish or defect.
—*1 Peter* 1:18–19

I have set before you life and death, blessings and curses. Now choose life, so that you and your children may live and that you may love the Lord your God, listen to his voice, and hold fast to him.
—*Deuteronomy* 30:19–20

For my husband, Michael, whose encouragement and unconditional love has allowed me to grow both as a writer and as a daughter of the king. We are the evidence that where you came from does not determine where you're going.

ONE

Sarah Langston winced as the barrel of the gun jabbed her stomach. The knit cap, turned backward on her head, made it impossible to see. She could feel the motion of the SUV, but she had no idea where her captors were taking her. Fear permeated every cell of her body.

The man with the gun leaned close and whispered in her ear. "Tell you what. We'll give you one more chance. You let us know where your brother is and we'll let you go."

He'd asked that question fifty times before. Always, her answer was the same. Why wouldn't they believe her?

Her voice trembled. "I told you. I don't know where Crew is. He's homeless. He contacts me when he wants to talk."

Her pulse drummed in her ears as her muscles tensed.

The second man, the driver, hadn't spoken for a long time. The tires made a different sound when they'd switched from paved roads to gravel. They'd left the city. Where were they going? What did they intend to do with her?

Both of them had been wearing masks when they'd grabbed her outside her home. They must have been waiting for the opportunity to catch her alone. More than once in the last day, she'd felt the invisible press of a gaze on her only to turn and see no one. Yesterday, she noticed the same Chevy Suburban parked outside the grocery store and at a friend's house. She'd dismissed it as coincidence.

In an attempt at escape, she'd managed to pull the mask off of one of the thugs, the skinny one with the bulging eyes. After that, they put the blindfold on her and drove without saying anything other than that same question, over and over again.

She could only guess at why they were looking for Crew. Her big brother was in and out of addiction, jobs and her life. Maybe he owed them money.

The sound of the tires rolling along changed. They were on a dirt road. Tension filled the silent car. Why were they driving so far out of town?

She knew then that the man had lied. They had no intention of letting her go.

The car rumbled to a stop but her thoughts continued racing. When she'd pulled the skinny one's mask off, he'd gone ballistic. The men had not wanted to be identified. They were taking her out of town to kill her, some place where her body wouldn't be found.

Sarah's mind moved at the speed of light. She had seconds to plan her escape. She'd been working to loosen the ties around her wrists.

Her car keys with the pepper spray attached were in her pocket. She coughed and turned her body slightly while she slipped her hand into her jacket pocket.

The man next to her jabbed her stomach with the gun. "Get out and don't try any funny business."

The front door opened. She heard footsteps and then the door closest to her squeaked open.

The driver spoke. "Come on, sweetheart."

Sarah scooted along the seat toward the open door. She tried to picture where the two men were. Judging from his voice, the driver had stepped away from her door.

The gun pressed against her back as she scooted along

the seat. Her fingers wrapped around the pepper spray slowly, carefully pulling it out of her pocket. Then in one quick movement, she turned and pressed the release button.

The groaning told her she'd hit her target. She tore off the knit hat and leapt out of the car.

An arm suctioned around her waist, and a hand slapped over her mouth. Her keys flew out of her hand, but she wasn't done fighting. She'd just have to use a different weapon. She bit down hard on the man's hand and felt a rush of triumph when he yelped and pulled his hand away. She scratched fingernails across the arm that held her waist. He didn't let go.

She elbowed him in the stomach, a hard swift jab.

His grip on her let up enough for her to angle away from him. Heart racing with fear and urgency, she ran toward the trees. Branches, sky and undergrowth were all a blur in front of her. Her sharp, rasping breathing enveloped her. Feet pounding, jumping over logs, pushing through the trees.

Please, God, help me get away.

The men behind her shouted, breaking branches, charging toward her. Their noise growing louder, closer, pressing on her.

Sarah pushed forward, willing her feet to move faster. Fighting off the terror that rose inside her, she stumbled into the clearing that bordered Bridger Lake. She only had a second to survey her surroundings before the men burst from the trees.

On instinct, she turned and ran toward the other part of the forest and the mountain beyond that. If she could make it up the mountain without being caught, maybe someone in the fire tower at the top of it could help her.

She prayed she'd make it that far.

* * *

From the high metal tower where he watched for forest fires, Bryan Keyes drew the binoculars up to his eyes and scanned the forest and the lake below. He studied the tree-covered mountains in the distance, searching for wisps of smoke. As dry as the summer had been, the tiniest fire could rage out of control within minutes. Anything out of the ordinary would draw his attention. In the few weeks that he had been here, he'd memorized every patch of trees, every cluster of rocks. The solitude and monotony of fire spotting was a far cry from his usual job as a police detective recently relocated to Discovery, Montana.

His stomach coiled into a tight knot. He didn't want to think about his work as a cop. He'd taken a leave of absence when doubt had crept in, and he'd started wondering if he could ever really make a difference. After months of work gathering the evidence that Tyler Mason was using his temp work agency for human trafficking and illegal labor, Mason had avoided going to trial.

Bryan stepped away from the windows that wrapped around the tower's octagonal structure. Even thinking about Tyler Mason put his nerves on edge. He wanted justice. Though he'd grown up in Discovery, Bryan had been a detective in Spokane for years. Tyler Mason lured unsuspecting immigrants and sentenced them to lives of hard labor and imprisonment all over the United States. When Bryan uncovered a slave labor factory in Spokane, his investigation led him to Tyler Mason who owned a home and a business in Discovery. In an effort to take down Mason, he'd requested a transfer five months ago.

But then a key witness had disappeared, and the case had fallen apart. And now, the department didn't want to expend any more time or manpower on what seemed like a battle they couldn't win.

Gritting his teeth, he studied the landscape. A dust

cloud on the road below indicated that a vehicle was headed toward Bridger Lake. Unusual to see people out here, considering how high the fire danger was. The metal of the car glinted in the late afternoon sun.

Bryan drew the binoculars back up to his face, watching as a man got out of the driver's side and opened the back door. A moment later, a woman jumped out. Bryan's back stiffened. The man grabbed the woman from behind, but she twisted away, running into the forest. The driver and a second man chased after her.

Bryan's heart pounded as he scanned the area, trying to get a clear view of what was going on. At this distance, it was hard to tell, but nothing about the interaction seemed friendly.

Finally, he spotted all three of them in the clearing by the lake.

He watched the man push the woman forward. The binoculars shook as Bryan focused in on the action. He was too far away to see clearly and the angle was all wrong, but it looked like the woman's hands were tied behind her back. He couldn't be sure.

He adjusted the focus hoping to see more. No luck. The woman's long brown hair hid her face as she trudged forward with her head down. Then just before the three of them disappeared into the trees, one of the men reached into the back of his waistband. Sunshine shone against the metal of the gun.

His breath hitched. They were going to shoot her.

Bryan dropped the binoculars as adrenaline surged through his body. The most direct route to the woman was straight down the nearly ninety-degree mountain, a hard five- to seven-minute run on rocky terrain to the lake where the armed men had parked. It was the only chance he had of getting there on time. Hiking out to his truck and then taking the circuitous route on logging roads would take an hour or more.

He regretted having turned in his police issue Glock, but the forest service provided a rifle in case of bear attacks. He grabbed it and bolted out the door and down the narrow metal stairs of the tower.

Holding the rifle with both hands, he scrambled down the mountainside. Rocks rolled in the wake of his hurried footsteps. No clear trail came into view. He'd grown up camping in these mountains and had developed pretty accurate radar for finding his way. He knew where the road connected to the lake, but would he get there in time?

As he ran, he listened for the crack of a gun being fired breaking through the thick August air. Silence surrounded him. Did that mean the woman was still alive?

He jumped over a boulder. The terrain became steeper, and he dug his heels in. His foot caught on a root and flung him forward. The rifle flew from his hands, clattering to a stop on a sheer cliff some twenty feet down. He could maneuver around the cliff, but there was no time to climb down and retrieve the rifle.

He forged ahead, praying that he'd be in time. He worked his way through the thick trees seeking an open path.

Bryan stopped, blood freezing in his veins when a gunshot shattered the serenity of the forest.

TWO

From the moment she'd pulled the mask off one of her abductors, Sarah had sensed that the hours of her life were numbered. Now as they dragged her deeper into the forest, she knew she was nearing the end. The men were not bothering with the masks anymore. Clear evidence that she wasn't coming out of this forest alive.

One of the men—the muscular one with the deep voice—pushed hard on her back. "Where is he?"

They still hadn't given up their line of questioning. Some sort of last-ditch effort to get the information they'd kidnapped her for in the first place. Their desperation and rage had escalated since her second escape attempt.

She spoke between gasps. "I…don't…know…where my brother is." Her wrists hurt from where the rope cut into her skin. This time they'd made sure her bindings were tight.

Deep Voice grabbed her hair, pulled her close and hissed in her ear. "You're his sister." He shoved her forward. "You should know."

Sarah stumbled from the force of the push. "He doesn't have a phone. He lives all over the place." Though she and her brother had been raised in foster care together, their lives had gone in very different directions. The last time she'd seen Crew, he had not been in good shape. He was sober, but rail-thin and shaking, probably from withdrawal.

"He talks about you," said the second kidnapper, a skinny man with acne scars whose eyes were still red from his dose of pepper spray. His words made Sarah frown. How well did Crew know these men? How had he gotten mixed up with people who were so clearly dangerous?

"I'm telling you, I haven't seen him in a month, and I don't know how to get in touch with him."

"You're lying." Deep Voice grabbed her arm at the elbow and swung her around, which made the rope dig even deeper into her wrist. "Where have you hidden him?"

She lowered her head and angled away from the criminal. "I'm not hiding him. Why won't you believe me?"

"You've got thirty seconds to tell me." She heard the slide on a gun click back. Even under the threat of death, she couldn't tell them. Why wouldn't they believe her?

"Yeah, stop protecting him." Acne Scars grabbed her shoulder and pushed her to the ground. She landed on her knees.

"Twenty seconds," said Deep Voice.

The menacing tone in his voice told her that he would have no qualms about shooting her.

Sarah closed her eyes. *Oh, God, please take me quickly.*

"Ten seconds."

Her whole body shook and she tasted bile. "I don't know where he is." Her voice was barely above a whisper. "I'm telling you the truth."

Please, God, send help. I don't want to die.

"Ten. Nine."

"You got anything to say?" said Acne Scars.

She shook her head. A cry rose up in her throat. "No, I can't tell you where he is because I don't know." Her stomach somersaulted. She couldn't contain her anguish. "Please believe me."

"Six. Five. Four."

As she leaned forward, every muscle in her body tensed. Tears formed. "Please."

"Three. Two. One."

She lurched at the boom of the gunshot as her body went rigid. No pain came. She took in a ragged breath.

She heard Deep Voice's harsh laughter. "That was a warning shot." Cold hard metal touched her temple. "Next time, it's for real. Put the blindfold back on her so she can't see it coming."

The hood went back over her head. A cold hand touched the back of her neck. The low voice was seductive. "Where is Crew Langston? Did you put him on a bus, help him get out of town?"

She shook her head, unable to form the words. Her heart pounded. She couldn't stop shaking.

"All right, lady, this is it." The hard gun barrel pressed against her temple.

Braced for another gunshot, she startled when she heard a thwacking sound, like a hard object making contact with flesh. One of the men groaned, and the gun was no longer pressed against her head. Flesh smacked against flesh. Men grunted. A body hit the ground close to her. Sarah struggled to get to her feet. Strong hands wrapped around her upper arm, warming her skin.

"Let's get you out of here and to a safe place." The voice sounded vaguely familiar. A hand grazed her forehead, lifting the hood off.

Her rescuer's eyes grew wide with recognition as her breath caught. Bryan Keyes. The man she thought she'd never see again. The man who had broken her heart into a thousand pieces.

The larger of the two assailants, curled up on the ground, stirred.

"Come on, we've gotta move. I'll cut you loose as soon

as I can." Bryan glanced around. He was probably looking for the gun or the best direction to run.

Acne Scars lay facedown, not moving. A log not too far from him must have been used to knock him out. But Deep Voice had started opening his eyes. They couldn't wait any longer—they needed to move.

Bryan must have reached the same conclusion because he shook his head and then pulled Sarah toward the trees. She ran, hindered by her hands still tied behind her back. Bryan held her arm to steady her.

He pulled her deeper into the trees until they came to a steep incline.

"No way can I climb that with my hands tied," she protested.

He glanced over his shoulder, pulled a pocketknife out of his worn jeans and cut the ropes that bound her wrists together.

"Better?" His fingers brushed over her wrist where the rope had dug in. Even after ten years, his touch had the power to make her heart flutter.

She stepped away. "Wait, what if we tried to get to the car they parked by the lake?" The shouts of Deep Voice barking orders to Acne Scars reached her ears.

"We'd run right into them." He scrambled partway up the rock and turned back, holding his hand out to her. She took his help. They climbed until they came to a steep rock face.

"I'll boost you up and then you can pull me up," he said.

Down below, she caught a flash of movement. Deep Voice was wearing a bright yellow shirt, easy to see amongst the evergreens. And easy to realize that he was catching up. "Where are you taking me?"

"Some place safe where we can call for help." He glanced down the mountain.

She hesitated.

"Trust me, I know this part of the forest," he said. "Come on, we can't stop." He laced his fingers together, indicating that she should put her foot in them.

What choice did she have? She'd prayed for God to send help and He had. Now it was up to her to make the most of it. Sarah put her foot in Bryan's hands. He pushed upward as she reached out for a handhold. God must have a sense of humor. Of all the people in the world, He'd sent Bryan. Ten years was a long time. She'd been a sophomore in high school and he a senior when they'd fallen in love. Or what passes for love in a sixteen-year-old's heart. She couldn't say now if she had loved him or had just been desperate to be loved. But at the time, it sure had felt real.

With Bryan pushing her up from below, she reached for a gnarled tree sprouting up close to the rock. She pulled herself up, gripping the tree with both hands. Bryan gave her a final push. She turned and reached down for him.

"I think I can get a foothold." He grabbed her hand, their eyes meeting momentarily.

The love between them had shattered when she became pregnant. They had agreed that the best thing for their little girl was adoption. But Bryan had been so angry afterward, had blamed her as though the decision hadn't been made together.

Bryan strained to get up the cliff face. "Other hand," he groaned.

She held both his hands and pulled as he struggled to get some traction with his feet. The muscles in her arms strained. "Almost there."

She pulled with all her strength, dragging him to the flat top of the cliff face. She leaned back, breathless from the exertion. Bryan scrambled to his feet.

"Come on." He held his hand out to her. The August sun beat down on them, the air thick with heat. Down below, the two thugs were weaving their way up the mountain, choosing an easier but less direct path.

"Where are we going, anyway?" Sarah still hadn't caught her breath.

"We need to get help, call the sheriff," he said.

She stared up at the rocky terrain. "Isn't there an easier way?"

"Sarah, would you trust me? I work here—I know where I'm going. Those guys won't be able to follow us. They'll give up."

It was the first time he'd said her name. The warmth in his voice only reminded her of ten-year-old wounds. "I really don't have a choice here. I'll do what you say." She wasn't so sure about the men giving up, though.

They crawled over rocks and through thick brush. A branch flicked across her forehead. She kept moving despite the stinging pain and the warm ooze of blood. The fire tower came into sight. So, he was some kind of forest ranger? By the time he'd left town to go to college, he hadn't spoken to her in months.

He led her up the narrow metal stairs into the tower, then stepped over to a small stand that contained the radio. He keyed the radio explaining that he needed a replacement and then said something about notifying the sheriff. He gave a brief but accurate description of the two thugs and their car.

While he talked, Sarah wandered around the sparse room. A double burner for cooking rested on a counter. Canned goods and gallons of water were stacked against the wall. An instrument of some sort with a map was in the dead center of the circular room. There was a desk and a chair in one corner, a cot in another. She sat down on the chair. A stack of books rested by the bed. He must stay up here weeks at a time. Yet, the place was utterly impersonal. Why had Bryan chosen such a solitary life? What had happened in the ten years since she'd seen him?

Bryan signed off and placed the radio back on the hook. He turned to face her. Those same warm brown eyes looked out at her, though they were edged with crow's-feet and worry lines now, and there was a hint of weariness in his expression that hadn't been there ten years ago. They had both been so naive and full of hope back then.

"What now?" She leaned forward, resting her elbows on her knees.

He walked over to the windows, picked up the binoculars and peered down the mountain. "We catch our breath."

"We wait?" Fear returned, sending a shock through her system. Those men meant to kill her.

"The forest service will notify the sheriff's department. They'll get those guys."

The memory of the gun pressed against her temple returned. Her throat constricted and her heart raced. "Do you think it's a good idea to just sit here?"

"We're not just sitting here." He handed her the binoculars. "Look, they've already left. I figured they would give up."

She walked over to the windows and peered through the binoculars at the shimmering water below. No car. She focused on the road where she saw the light-colored SUV heading away from the lake. So he was right. "Can they drive up here?"

"It will take them over an hour. And if they don't know these roads, they'll never find us." His voice was filled with reassurance.

Sarah let out a breath, relaxing a little.

He leaned close to her and touched her forehead where the tree branch had cut the skin. "I've got something for that. Go sit down." He pointed toward the cot.

Sarah put the binoculars down and wandered to the cot.

She tried to take in a deep breath. Those men had meant to kill her. Would they give up that easily? After grabbing the first-aid kit from a storage box, Bryan walked across the room and sat close to her. She could feel his body heat.

He handed her a piece of leather. "Tie your hair back, so it's out of the way."

She gathered her hair into a ponytail.

He pulled disinfectant out of the first-aid kit and touched the end of the tube lightly to her forehead. "It's going to be okay, but we should get moving. After I deal with this cut, we'll hike over to my truck."

She closed her eyes as he gently pressed the bandage against her forehead. Memories of his touch all those years ago awakened old feelings. The power of the attraction made her forget the pain of how everything had ended... for a moment.

"There's a little country store eight miles up the road. You can call for a friend to come and get you." He wadded up the packaging the bandage had come in. "By that time, the sheriff will catch those guys."

The warm feelings evaporated. So he meant to ditch her as quickly as he could, just like old times. He'd only been doing his duty. It was the kind of person he was. But now that his duty was finished, he wanted nothing more to do with her. "I suppose I should go to the police." She hoped her voice didn't give away the hurt she felt.

"Yeah, you'll want to report this." His voice was tainted with a bitterness she didn't understand. "But not to the city police. This happened in the county. You'll want to talk to the sheriff."

"But they grabbed me at my house...in town."

He rose to his feet and ran his fingers through his wavy brown hair. He spoke without turning back to look at her. "If you don't mind my asking, why were those guys trying to kill you? What did you do?"

His tone was disconcerting. Did he actually think she was mixed up with something illegal? It had been a sore spot with them when they dated. His parents had never thought she was good enough for their football star son. His lawyer mother and business-owner father viewed her as the girl from the wrong side of the tracks. By that time, Crew was already having problems, too.

It didn't matter that she had been a good student and never been in trouble. She didn't have the wrong pedigree. She had no pedigree.

She took a deep breath and idly picked up one of the books in his stack. "They were looking for Crew."

Bryan's face brightened. "How is Crew?"

"I wish I could tell you. He has a drug and alcohol habit. Sometimes he has a place to live, sometimes not." Now she was the one who sounded bitter. Crew, two years older than her, had been her protector when they were kids. But years of having to be an adult too soon had worn him down. He'd started out a petty thief and picked up a drug habit along the way.

Bryan stroked his chin. "I always liked Crew. I liked the way he looked out for you."

Sarah felt a stab to her heart. Crew had made bad choices; she knew that. But the image that burned in her mind of her brother was of him offering her his last morsel of bread when they'd run away from an abusive foster home and hidden in the forest. Her heart warmed toward Bryan that he could remember the most positive thing about Crew, the reason she still loved her brother.

"I keep hoping he'll turn things around." And she wouldn't give up that hope no matter how bad things looked.

Bryan stepped away from the window. "Sometimes people do, you know. Get their lives together." He rested his gaze on her long enough to make her feel self-conscious. His look could still send an electric charge through her.

Sarah glanced down at the book she had picked up. C. S. Lewis, one of her favorite authors. But what was Bryan doing with a book like this? He'd never been interested in books with faith messages when she'd known him. Maybe his comment about people getting their lives together had been as much about himself as her brother. She hoped so. She'd found faith at the home where she stayed while she was pregnant. She'd gotten her life back on track at Naomi's Place. Maybe somewhere along the road Bryan had had a similar transformation. She'd never stopped praying for him.

She put the book back on the stack. "We should get going."

"Yeah, it's a little bit of a hike to get to the truck." Bryan walked across the room. "Do you want a drink of water before we go?"

She rose to her feet and stared out the windows that provided a panoramic view of the forest. "My throat is dry." She still couldn't figure out why Bryan would choose such a lonely job. He'd always been so outgoing. "How long do you stay up here at a time?"

Bryan lifted one of the gallon containers of water to the desk and retrieved a cup. "Three weeks on and one week off."

She crossed her arms and stared down at the rocks and forest they had climbed through to get here. She saw a flash of yellow and then Deep Voice stepped free of the thick forest. His gaze traveled up toward the tower. Panic pulsed through her. "Bryan, I think we have a problem."

THREE

Adrenaline flooded through Bryan's body. The thug charged straight for them at a steady and intense pace. He was the bigger of the two men, muscular to an excess. The short, thin man must have taken off in the vehicle, maybe planning on taking the winding road that would eventually bring him to the other side of the fire-lookout tower in case his friend didn't make it up the mountainside. It was a rookie mistake for Bryan to assume they'd both left in the SUV. He'd been too distracted by Sarah to think straight—and he was paying for that now.

"What do we do?" The fear in Sarah's voice intensified.

His mind catapulted from one possibility to another. She was the prime target. He had to get her out of here.

Bryan flipped open the glass door that led to the catwalk, grabbed a length of rope and tied it off on the central post in the tower. "He'll come up the stairs. You slip off this side of the tower. Go due east, and you'll see a trail that leads to an open area. My truck is there."

"But what about you?"

The look in her eyes was wild. She was so afraid. He longed to take her in his arms, but after all they had been through ten years ago, would she even accept his comfort? "I'll hold him off." He walked over to a box and pulled out a set of keys which he handed to her. "Go to town and get help. I'll be all right."

She shook her head. "We should stay together."

"Go, Sarah. I can handle this guy." He pushed her toward the door. They didn't have time for a discussion.

She grabbed the rope, stepped out on the catwalk and moved to the edge of the tower. Her gaze locked on to him, longing filling her eyes. He'd seen that look before. She'd been a strong, resourceful young woman when he'd met her. But there was a vulnerable side to Sarah that stayed hidden from most people.

He pressed his hands against her face, kissed her forehead. "Go. You'll be fine."

The look of fear and doubt remained as she shook her head.

"And I'll be okay, too," he added.

She nodded, though the worry lines in her forehead intensified. She slipped off the side of the tower and disappeared from view.

He raced over to the radio. Where was his replacement? Had the sheriff made it out to the road by the lake and stopped the thug in the car? He had to let the authorities know what was happening. Before he could reach anyone, he heard the sound of footsteps on the stairs.

The fire tower door had no lock. He could buy Sarah precious minutes by holding this guy off. He'd taken down him and his cohort once before. This time it was only one man.

The footsteps intensified, grew louder.

Bryan grabbed a steak knife. There was no closet, no place to hide and try to get the jump on the guy…or was there? He crawled out on the catwalk and pulled himself to the roof just as the door burst open.

He pressed flat against the roof, angling his head so he could see through the skylight. Maybe the assailant would look around, figure they hadn't come to the fire tower and leave. That would be the best case scenario. He'd be able to catch up with Sarah and make sure she got safely into town.

From this angle he could see the top of the man's head. There was a pistol in his hand. So, he had found the gun.

The thug surveyed the room. Then he noticed the open door where Sarah had escaped. Bryan cringed. In his haste, he'd forgotten to close it.

The assailant stomped through the open door that led to the catwalk. He studied the rope where Sarah had descended.

With his belly pressed against the roof, Bryan swung around, head facing downward on the slanted roof. Sarah should be emerging into an open section of the forest. If the thug looked in that direction, he would see her and know where she'd gone.

Bryan slid down the roof. The man looked up but had no time to brace himself before Bryan leapt on top of him, knocking him to the ground and breaking a section of the railing around the catwalk. Both men recovered and rose to their feet. Bryan was relieved to notice that the assailant had dropped his gun in the struggle. The narrow catwalk provided little room to maneuver. Bryan struck the man across the face, hoping to throw him off balance.

The man had a square jaw and eyes like slits. His lip curled back, revealing large teeth. He lunged toward Bryan. If he could get an upper hand, find a way to subdue him and restrain him, the sheriff could question him and find out why they were after Sarah's brother.

"Where is the Langston woman?" The man barreled toward him.

Bryan dodged, but slipped off the edge of the catwalk where the railing had broken free. He fell to the rocky ground below. It took him a moment to recover. When he looked up, he couldn't see the man.

On hands and knees he scrambled to the base of the tower. The overhang of the catwalk shielded him from view. He worked his way around the tower back to the stairs.

Grabbing a thick branch for a weapon, he crept up the stairs. The door was slightly ajar. Peeking around it, he was rewarded with a quick image of the thug staring at the floor. He was looking for the gun. Bryan watched until the man's back was turned. He pushed the door open and landed a blow across the man's shoulders.

The thug groaned in pain, turned and swung for Bryan. Bryan hit him a second time on the arm with the log before the man wrenched it free. The two men wrestled. The assailant was twice his size, but Bryan refused to back down. Slowing this man down was the only chance Sarah would have to escape. They exchanged blows, drawing nearer to the open door.

Bryan lifted his arm, hand curled into a fist, ready to land a hit. The solid surface beneath his feet evaporated. He tumbled backward down the stairs. Like being smacked over and over, he could feel the hits to his body on the way down. He stopped at the bottom, still conscious, but disoriented. The assailant hadn't come after him. He heard the sound of things being moved around inside the fire tower. He was still looking for the gun and probably assumed Bryan was unconscious or dead.

Bryan wasn't sure if he could move. Had he broken any bones? Every muscle felt like it had been cut or bruised. He sat up. Pain shot through his body. It hurt to breathe. He needed to hide. He couldn't fight in his current state. But no, he couldn't back down, either. The assailant wouldn't give up until he found out where Sarah was. Bryan tried to push himself to his feet.

The noise inside stopped. The thug came to the top of the stairs. He lifted the gun, taking aim. "Where is she?"

By force of will, Bryan scrambled to his feet. He stumbled toward the shelter of the trees. He was pretty beat up. He probably couldn't outrun the thug, but he could hide, maybe draw the man into chasing after him instead of Sarah. He stepped into the trees and onto the trail.

Sarah appeared. A look of shock flashed across her features when she saw him. He had bruises on his arms. She grabbed him. "I couldn't leave without you." She wrapped her arm around his waist. The first shot from the thug's gun pierced the air. "We'd better hurry."

As she held on to him, he could feel his strength returning. Nothing was broken. He may have bruised a rib. He was in shock and badly beat up, but not to the point where he couldn't move quickly. They ran along the trail. A second shot broke off a tree branch in front of them.

They came to the clearing where the truck sat. "I can drive," Bryan said.

Sarah hesitated, drawing the keys close to her chest.

"It's not as bad as it looks," said Bryan.

She handed him the keys and sprinted around the truck to the passenger-side door. He climbed into the cab, started the engine and closed the door just as the assailant came into the clearing. Bryan hit the gas doing a tight turn to get out of the parking area. The back tires spat out gravel as a bullet collided with metal.

Sarah craned her neck. "I think he hit the side of the truck."

He'd probably been aiming for the tires. Bryan pressed the accelerator to the floor. He didn't want to give this guy a second chance. The truck jolted and lumbered down the mountain road.

Sarah leaned back against the seat, tilting her head. Her curly brown hair had worked free of the ponytail. Her face was covered with sweat and dirt. She turned her head, soft blue eyes resting on him. She'd come back for him, risked her life. "He won't be able to catch us now. Not on foot."

"Yeah." He didn't want to worry her about the second hit man. Had the sheriff made it to the car or had the thug gotten away?

"How far is it to this country store?"

"I'll take you all the way into town…and to the police station." He didn't like the idea of leaving her anywhere until he could be assured she was safe, though he dreaded the thought of returning to the police station. His departure had not been a quiet one. Incensed at the lack of justice over Tyler Mason, he'd let his chief know how he felt.

"Thank you for doing that." Sarah leaned back and closed her eyes.

He reached over and patted her leg without thinking. It was a gesture he'd done a thousand times when they were dating. She sat up straight, and her eyes popped open.

He bit the inside of his cheek. What a stupid move. Of course, he didn't think he could go back to where they had been ten years ago. Too much had changed, even before they parted ways.

He cleared his throat. "We do need to stop at the country store and make some phone calls. My cell phone is back at the fire tower. I need to find out if my replacement made it." He hated abandoning his post and worried that he'd sent his replacement into a dangerous situation if the guy was still skulking around the woods with a gun. Though he doubted the thug would hurt anyone else and risk having another person who could identify him.

The road evened out, decreasing the bouncing in the truck. Sarah folded her hands in her lap as a tense silence fell between them.

What did they talk about now? What *could* they talk about that wouldn't open old wounds? Even thinking about how their relationship had ended made his chest tight. No, he couldn't go there again.

Sarah leaned toward him and pointed through the windshield. "That must be it, huh?"

A hundred yards ahead was a concrete building with a parking lot full of trailers. As they neared the store, signs advertising raft and boat rentals and bait for sale came into view. A campground a mile up the road was the main source of business for the store along with the abundance of fishermen who came for the freshwater fishing. Bryan pulled into the dirt lot.

"It'll take me just a minute to make these calls," Bryan said.

Sarah nodded. The bandage above her eye had come lose. He reached over and pressed it against her forehead.

She lifted her chin as a show of resolve. She'd always been a strong person emotionally. She had had to be. But what she had been through today would have made anyone fall apart. He touched her cheek with his knuckles. "It's going to be okay. I'll get you into town." She nodded and tried to smile. Bryan resisted the urge to pull her into a comforting hug. It wasn't his place to do that for her anymore.

Bryan got out of the truck and ambled toward the store entrance.

Alone in the truck, Sarah glanced out the back window. A hard, cold mass of fear had settled in her chest. These men were not going to give up easily. What could Crew have done for this kind of wrath to come down on him? He must have gone into hiding or the men wouldn't have sought her out. Wherever he was, she hoped he was safe.

She looked out Bryan's window. Mixed in with all the trailers, there was only one car parked off to the side that must belong to the owner or store clerk. No one wandered around outside. Through the store window, she could see Bryan step up to the counter while the clerk rang up his purchases.

She would have been dead by now if it hadn't been for Bryan. How had a forest ranger learned to fight like that? She placed her fingers on the bandage on her forehead. His gentle touch had caused memories of being held by him to rise to the surface. All those years ago, she'd rested her head on his chest surrounded by his heartbeat while strong arms enveloped her. Back then, she had felt safe for the first time in her life when she was with him. But it didn't last.

Bryan emerged from the store holding two large cans. She leaned over and opened the door for him. He handed her one of the cans, an iced tea. "That drink I meant to get for you earlier."

Moved by such a small act of consideration, she opened the can and took a sip. The cool liquid traveled smoothly down her parched throat. She took several more gulps. "That tastes really good, thanks."

Bryan sat behind the wheel, popped the tab on his tea and placed it in the cup holder. "My replacement made it to the tower. No sign of the guy with the gun. I checked in with the sheriff and called the city police, too. They might be willing to get involved since the kidnapping took place in town. You can make your statement to them."

"Did the sheriff say if they caught the other guy?" She shivered despite the heat, not wanting to think about those men being on the loose.

Bryan started the truck. "The dispatcher hadn't heard anything. She's gonna send the deputy up to the tower to make sure the area is clear."

For a forest ranger, Bryan seemed to know a lot about how the police worked. She had to know what he'd been doing for the past ten years. "So did you go to college like you planned?"

Bryan's head jerked back and he laughed. He pulled out of the dirt parking lot. "Boy, that question came out of nowhere."

"I was just curious." It was the first mention either of them had made of the past.

Bryan's truck came to a crossroads. He turned onto a paved two-lane. "I…ah…started out that semester, but it was a little too much for me to handle." Each word was wrought with tension.

Sarah crossed her arms and stared out the window. His discomfort made it clear that even such a benign question was off limits. She wondered, too, how and why he had ended up back in Discovery, but now she didn't dare ask. She longed to have a normal conversation with him, but that wasn't going to happen. It would be best if he just dropped her off at the police station. He could go back out to his lonely fire tower. If they ran into each other in town, they could keep the conversation to hello and the weather.

Bryan glanced at the rearview mirror. "What's this guy's problem?"

Sarah turned around to look at the SUV following too closely. Shock spread through her. "Bryan, that's the vehicle."

He glanced a second time just as the Suburban tapped their bumper.

"He must have been waiting for us." Bryan pressed the gas. "Knowing this was the only road that led into town."

"How could he know this was your truck?"

"I don't know. Maybe he was watching the store. Maybe he has a way to communicate with the other guy." Bryan pulled away from the Suburban only to have it catch up with them again. The car bumped the back of the truck again, causing it to lurch.

"Hold on." Bryan executed a sudden turn onto a dirt road.

The other car overshot the turn, but spun around and charged up the road toward them. Bryan turned off into a grassy field and veered back to the main road, but in the wrong direction—away from town.

The car caught up to them. Bryan gripped the steering wheel as the Suburban came alongside them and smashed against his truck. Metal crunched. The truck wobbled, but Bryan kept it on the road.

The second hit was harder. The Suburban seemed to be attached to the passenger side of the truck as it pushed them closer to the edge of the road.

Sarah looked through her window at the leering, maniacal face of Acne Scars, as their truck was pushed off the road toward the rocky incline below.

FOUR

Their truck flew off the road at a high speed, sailed through the air and landed in the river at the bottom of the rocky incline. Sarah gasped for air as the truck settled and water rose up around it. She felt as if every muscle in her body had been stretched, and her thoughts seemed to move in slow motion.

Sarah turned toward Bryan whose head was tilted at an unnatural angle. Panicked, she fumbled with her seat belt and reached over to shake him. "Bryan!" She wrapped her hand around his muscular upper arm. "Bryan, please."

He stirred, shaking his head and moaning in pain. She let out a breath. He was alive.

Bryan glanced from side to side as though trying to fathom what had happened. She reached across his stomach and unbuckled his seat belt.

The current propelled the car downriver. The metal frame creaked as the water pushed against it.

"We need to get out of here, right?"

He looked at her, blinking several times. "Yeah...yeah." His eyes were void of comprehension.

"Or would it be better to drift with the current?" The truck picked up speed and turned sideways.

He looked around. "No." His gaze became more focused. "The water gets deeper, more rapids."

"I think we are closer to the bank on my side." She glanced out the back window. Acne Scars's Suburban must have pushed with so much force that it too had sailed off the road and landed upside-down on the rocky shore.

She rolled down her window. Water seeped into the cab of the truck.

"Hurry," said Bryan. "Swim as hard as you can to shore. The current is pretty strong. I'll be right behind you."

She pushed herself through the window into the cold river. Rushing, swirling water suctioned around her. The cold of it shocked her into stillness for a moment as the force of the current pulled her under. She swallowed water and panic surged. She fought against it, struggling to the surface. She pierced the water with her hand, keeping her eyes on the bank which seemed to be slipping farther away.

She caught a quick glimpse of Bryan as he drifted downriver. He was pretty banged up from his fight, and he'd lost consciousness in the wreck. Was he in any condition to make a swim like this? His head went under as an awful sense of dread filled her.

I can't lose him.

She crashed into a submerged log. She was able to catch her breath by grabbing on to one of the larger branches that stuck out of the water. Holding her position, she desperately scanned the water for a glimpse of Bryan, breathing a sigh of relief when his head bobbed to the surface as he stroked toward the shore, his movement steady and strong.

She pulled herself along the top of the log and then pushed off, aiming for the shore. Up ahead she could see the rapids—foaming, intense waves cresting and swirling. Terror spread through her. No way did she have the strength to swim through those. She needed to get to land. She jabbed her arm through the water, though her muscles had grown weak from the struggle. Her legs felt heavy.

Rivers, just like oceans, had an undertow. The closer

she got to the rapids the bigger the risk of being pulled under and drowned.

The shore grew nearer inch by inch. The water calmed as she struggled toward an eddy. This time, when she put her feet down, she touched bottom. *Thank You, God.* Sarah dragged herself to the shore and crumpled onto a sandbar.

She heard footsteps and turned her head sideways. Bryan had gotten ashore farther upriver. He ran toward her, looking over his shoulder and then increasing his pace. The look of fear on his face fueled her panic. Sarah sat up.

He reached down and grabbed her arm. "We've got company. Come on."

Acne Scars must have gotten out of the SUV. Sarah had barely caught her breath when Bryan lifted her to her feet and pulled her toward the thick brush. Both of them were soaking wet. Their shoes squished as they ran. Her wet clothes, which weighed an extra five pounds, slapped against her body. She was grateful for the warmth of the sun. They'd dry off quick enough.

Bryan led her through the thickness of the forest. The canopy reduced the light by half, and the temperature dropped ten degrees.

"Where...are...we...going?" Sarah spoke as she ran, taking a breath after each word.

"Back to the store. We can call for help from there. The sheriff will have to meet us and escort us back to town."

The forest thinned. They came to the steep incline that led back up to the road. Only prairie grass grew on this side of the hill. Bryan scanned the area above them. "This is the only way to get to the road. We'll be exposed as we go."

Sarah took in a breath to push down the rising fear. "If it's the only way."

"Stay behind me." Bryan made the steep trek with ease, continually glancing side to side and up above.

Sarah scrambled to keep up with him. She could see the

road not more than twenty yards above them. How much farther to the store after that?

Bryan stopped suddenly, his eyes growing wide. He turned and pulled her to the ground, placing a protective arm across her back. A zinging sound followed by an explosive echo shattered the silence of the forest.

Panic made her voice shake. "He has a rifle. Where did he get a rifle?"

"He probably had it with him in that car." From the ground where they lay, he turned to face her, reached out a hand and smoothed her wet hair back from her face. "It's going to be okay."

The tenderness of his voice was a soothing balm to her anxious, fear-filled thoughts.

"We'll get to that store," he assured her. "Stay low. The high grass will provide some cover."

They crawled the remaining distance to the road taking an indirect path. Still lying on his belly, Bryan lifted his head and peered over the asphalt then back down the hill.

He tugged on her wet shirt. "Follow the road but use the slope of the bank for cover. We should be safe."

Sarah took in a breath to calm her nerves. Her heart still hadn't stopped racing.

Why was this happening? What kind of trouble had Crew gotten himself into? This had to be something more serious than an unpaid debt.

Bryan must have picked up on her fear. He grabbed her hand and pressed it between his. "We're almost there."

She nodded. They ran, crouched over until the store came into view. At that point, Bryan straightened, grabbed her hand and sprinted the remaining distance. Sarah glanced over her shoulder at the forest beyond the road.

As they neared the store, the windows looked dark. The car that had been parked on the side of the building earlier was gone. Sarah slowed her pace. The store was closed.

"Now what?"

Bryan surveyed the parking lot. "We've got to break in. We can leave a note, letting them know what happened. Maybe they have an alarm system that will bring help out here."

He trotted around to the side of the building, picked up a rock and smashed the glass on the side door. No alarm sounded. Bryan reached through the broken glass and unlatched the door. "Not exactly high security."

They stepped into what looked like a combination storage and break room. All it held was a Formica table with mismatched chairs, a coffeemaker and a shelf lined with canned goods, paper towels and boxes of fishing lures. They secured the door behind them as best they could, then with Bryan taking the lead, they walked into the darkened main part of the store.

Sarah reached for the light switch. Bryan grabbed her hand and shook his head. Sarah's gaze traveled to the large window at the front of the store.

A percussive boom shattered the air as the glass in the window splintered into a thousand pieces spraying everywhere. Sarah screamed and dove to the floor.

Bryan dragged her toward the protection of the checkout area. He kept one arm around her while he reached up to the top of the counter and pulled the phone down. "We can't wait for the sheriff." The beeps from him pressing the numbers seemed to come on top of each other. "Jake, how fast can you get to the bait store on River Road? I'm in some serious trouble here. Armed man on the perimeter. Bring extra firepower if you've got it….Good."

Sarah pressed her back against a cupboard. "Who was that?"

"A friend. He lives close. He'll get here faster than the cops."

"Why didn't you call the police?"

Bryan's expression hardened. "They've got a pretty lousy track record so far today."

She grabbed Bryan's shirt and glanced toward the broken window. "That guy knows we're in here. We don't have much time."

"Which is why we're not staying in here." Bryan opened and closed the drawers and cupboards on the checkout counter, clearly searching for something. "Sometimes they have a gun for protection." He opened one more drawer before giving up. He looked at her. "Make a run for the back door. Open it as little as possible. I'll be right behind you."

Questions raced through Sarah's head—How would the friend find them if they left the store? Wasn't there a risk that the friend would be shot, too?—but she knew it wasn't the time to ask them.

Sarah crawled toward the back door, reaching up to work the latch. She glanced back at the shattered window. The shooter wasn't in view, but that didn't mean he couldn't see them leaving the store. He had to be hiding in the trees across the road. She eased the door open to a narrow slit and squeezed through. Bryan pressed close to her back as they made their way along the outside wall of the store.

"Over there," he whispered, pointing to one of the boats for rent. He scrambled toward it and lifted a corner of the canvas cover. "Get in."

When she came to the end of the boat, she saw that a shed concealed it from view of the trees where Acne Scars likely hid. Sarah crawled through and lay down on the bottom of the boat, positioning her feet underneath the seat. Bryan crawled in beside her, reaching up to move the canvas cover back into place.

Lying on his side, he turned toward her and whispered, "Stay quiet. Jake's car has a loud engine. We'll hear it coming. We need to jump out and be ready to get in when he arrives."

She nodded, wondering when her heart rate would return to normal. She knew it wouldn't be any time soon when he lay close enough for her to feel his breath on her cheek. She inhaled his faint musk scent and looked into his deep brown eyes. The minutes ticked by. She dared not move.

A door slammed. She gasped. Bryan placed a calming hand on her shoulder. Footsteps crunched on gravel, growing closer. Every muscle in her body remained frozen. Her heartbeat drummed in her ears. Warmth radiated from her shoulder where Bryan's hand remained.

The footsteps passed by the boat and then stopped. She dared not take a breath. If Acne Scars tore the cover off the boat, they'd both be dead in an instant. A century went by before the footsteps resumed.

Bryan squeezed her shoulder. She turned her head to see him better. For a long moment, they lay in silence facing each other. She used to think she could drown in the deep brown of his eyes.

He motioned with his eyes. At first, she didn't know what he was trying to say. Then she heard it, the distant rumble of an engine.

This plan was fraught with risk. Was the killer lying in wait in the store? Had he returned to his post in the trees or had he assumed they'd run back into the forest and left altogether? There was no way to know.

The engine noise became more distinct. Bryan reached up to flip back the cover. He lifted his head above the rim of the boat and then pulled himself out. She rolled toward the edge of the boat and sat up.

"Hurry, we don't have much time."

She jumped to the ground and followed him as he raced toward the shed, pressing his back against it. She leaned close to him, holding on to his muscular arm. The car engine sounded like it was on top of them.

"Now, now." He pulled her toward the parking lot. The car was still twenty yards away. The first rifle shot kicked up rocks in front of them. The car zoomed into the lot at a high speed, turning a hundred and eighty degrees. The second rifle shot hit the side view mirror.

Bryan yanked open the back door, pulling Sarah ahead of him so she could get in first. A bullet hit the door as Bryan crawled inside. He slammed the door shut. The car stirred up gravel, swerved and sped down the road.

FIVE

By the time they had reached the outskirts of Discovery, Sarah's heart rate had mostly returned to normal. Though she kept glancing over her shoulder expecting to be fired at, she could manage a deep breath.

Bryan hadn't said anything on the ride into town other than to ask her if she was okay and introduce her to Jake. They sat close together in the backseat, their shoulders touching. What they had been through left them both speechless though she found some comfort in having him close. Bryan seemed to take his own comfort from the handgun that rested on his thigh.

As soon as they had gotten into the car, Jake had tossed it back to Bryan. Another gun sat on the front seat of the Dodge Charger. Bryan kept up a steady vigil of checking all the windows at intervals. From his actions, he too worried they would be attacked again. Even though she knew both of the men who had come after them were now on foot, the fear settled in her belly like a heavy rock.

She'd almost died today. And all because of something Crew had done. Sarah closed her eyes and tried to make sense of it all, but nothing seemed to fit. Yes, her brother had been in trouble before, but she knew he had a good heart. How had he gotten mixed up with those thugs? She'd seen the level of violence these men were capable of. Her heart squeezed tight. What if the sheriff didn't catch those men? What would they do to her brother when they found him? She had to get to Crew before those thugs did.

Jake slowed the car as he came within the city limits. He was a burly man with salt-and-pepper hair. He dressed in army surplus fatigues and smelled like cigars. She guessed he might be in his mid-fifties.

What kind of life did Bryan lead that he knew men who had access to guns at a moment's notice?

Bryan tensed as they drew nearer to the police station. Jake pulled into the parking lot, and they all exited the car.

Bryan slapped Jake on the back as they gripped hands. "Thanks, you saved my life."

"That makes us about even," said Jake. "You can take it from here?"

Bryan raised a leery eye toward the police station. "I'll be all right."

Jake got back into his car as Bryan escorted Sarah up the sidewalk. Sarah glanced back at the rough-looking man getting into his car. "So how do you know Jake?"

"We worked together on a case when I came here. Then he took early retirement."

A case? She wanted to ask what case he'd have worked on as a forest ranger, but the bitterness embedded in Bryan's words indicated he didn't want to tell her anything else.

Inside the station, only a few officers sat at computers. A series of cupboards, some of them locked, took up one wall of the police station. At the far end of the long, narrow room was an office with a window. The sign on the door read Chief Sandoval. Radios and scanners buzzed on and off throughout the station.

All of the men and the one woman working at their computers raised their head when Bryan stepped inside.

The officer closest to the door said, "Hey, Bryan."

The greeting was neither friendly nor hostile.

Bryan looked at one officer and then another. "Have you guys heard anything about what happened on Fire Mountain today?"

"I picked some things up on the scanner," said the female officer. "Don't think County ever caught up with those guys."

Sarah cringed. That meant they were still out there. At least it was a long walk into town.

Bryan rested a hand on her shoulder. "This is Sarah Langston. She's the woman who was abducted and almost killed today. She needs to make a statement, and we'll have her look at mug shots. She can identify her attackers and so can I."

"I'll get right on that. Just give me a second to set things up." The female officer scooted back her chair and disappeared around a corner.

From the familiarity that Bryan had with the other officers, it was clear he had some sort of connection to the police. "So how does a guy in a fire tower have such a cozy relationship with the city police?"

"I used to work here." Bryan angled his head, not making eye contact. He shifted his weight from one foot to the other.

Sarah stepped a little closer to him. "Used to?"

His expression turned hard as granite. "It's a long story." His voice became thick with emotion. "And not one I want to tell."

Even though she knew his anger was over whatever had happened on the job, his retort stung—a reminder of a much more personal anger that he had directed at her ten years ago. When she'd found out she was pregnant, they'd gone to a pregnancy counseling center. Naomi's Place had been warm and filled with love, a safe place for teens to live while they were pregnant. They both had agreed that giving up their little girl was the best choice for everyone. But after Bryan signed away his parental rights, he became sullen. His silent rage had made her feel like he blamed her for not wanting to keep their child. It didn't make sense. They had made the decision together. They didn't get a chance to talk things out. Instead, he left. His parents moved away shortly after.

In the two years after Bryan left, she had been adopted by a loving family. The adoption had come too late for Crew, who was past eighteen and already descending into his life of crime, but it had helped cement Sarah's resolve to take her life in a different direction. She too had left for college to get a degree in social work. She'd returned because she loved Discovery, because Crew and her adoptive parents were here, and maybe somewhere in the back of her mind she hoped Bryan would come back, as well.

Now he *was* back. But whatever he'd been doing, the years had not been kind to Bryan Keyes. The vulnerable teenager she had known was lost to a man with an eight-foot wall around his heart. And she had no desire to try to climb over it.

The female officer returned. "Why don't you come this way? I've set up an interview room for you. It'll be easier to concentrate in there." She held out her hand. "I'm Officer O'Connor, but you can call me Bridget."

Sarah stepped toward Bridget. Fear rose up. She didn't want to think about those two men. She glanced back at Bryan. "Can Bryan come with me?"

The officer spoke gently. "I have to take your statements separately."

"It'll be all right." He reached out and squeezed her upper arm. "Bridget has a very gentle bedside interrogation technique."

His joke made her smile.

Bridget opened a door labeled Interview Room One. "Right in here."

Sarah took in a deep breath. Tension wove around her chest at the prospect of having to relive the terror of the last few hours.

And worst of all was her certainty that it still wasn't over.

The look of vulnerability Bryan saw in Sarah's eyes as she turned the corner nearly tore his heart out. She was still shaken, still afraid. If he could just hold her. He remembered the softness of her skin and the light floral scent of her hair. Heat rose up his neck. Even after ten years, the memory held a power over him.

All the more reason for him to keep some distance between them now. He wouldn't do her any favors if he got distracted by the past. Only by staying focused on the danger could he truly help her.

He couldn't make the interview any easier for her, but maybe he could make sure those guys didn't come after her again. Once the thugs got back into town, Sarah would still be in danger unless Crew came forward.

Bryan looked through the window where Chief Sandoval sat hunched over his desk. Overwhelmed with frustration as the case against Tyler Mason dissolved, his parting words to his boss weeks ago had been harsh.

He understood why Sandoval had no desire to waste manpower and resources trying to find a new angle on the investigation. Mason did such a good job of playing the part of a fine upstanding businessman that most people fell for his act. Unless they could get another eyewitness to Mason's human trafficking ring who could put the finger on Mason, they really didn't have a case.

A tightness embedded in Bryan's chest as he walked toward Sandoval's glass office. The older man raised his head and peered through the window, giving away nothing in his expression.

Bryan tapped on the door.

"Come in."

"Sir?"

Sandoval leaned back in his chair. "Have you decided to put that badge back on, Officer Keyes?"

Bryan shook his head. If his job wasn't about getting justice, he wasn't so sure it was a job he wanted.

Sandoval's chair creaked as he leaned forward and rested his elbows on his desk. "Too bad, you're a good officer."

The compliment warmed him. Whatever conflict they had had, Sandoval was a competent chief. "I need to talk to you about another matter."

Sandoval nodded. "Go ahead."

"There's a woman in the interview room with Bridget right now. I witnessed two men try to kill her earlier today. I think her life is still in danger. She can identify them."

Sandoval straightened the papers on his desk. "So you think they will come for her again?"

"They were pretty relentless up on the mountain. Can we set her up with some protection?"

"Why were these men after her?" Not showing a high level of interest, Sandoval glanced at his computer monitor. "What does this relate to?"

"They wanted to know the whereabouts of her brother."

"Is the brother a criminal?"

Bryan was uncomfortable with the classification—the Crew he knew had been a good person, just on a bad path. "He has a history of drug use," Bryan admitted.

"So this might be about a bad debt or stolen drugs." Sandoval seemed distracted as he rose from his chair and opened a file cabinet drawer.

"We don't know. My gut says it's more serious than that.

These guys were pretty persistent. Sarah's not involved in drug culture—if they were going to kill her to send a message to her brother then it seems like more is at stake here than a simple debt."

"I can't spare an officer to provide 24/7 protection, but I can send an extra patrol through her neighborhood at night. The dispatcher can be made aware if a call does come from her home." He slammed the file drawer shut.

That wouldn't be enough to keep Sarah safe, but pressuring Sandoval would not be effective. "I appreciate that, sir." He turned to go. If the department couldn't protect Sarah, maybe he'd have to.

He wandered back through the station. The female officer who had been with Sarah walked toward him holding a computer printout. "Thought you might want to look at this. These are the two men she identified."

Bryan studied the photographs. "Yeah. Those are the guys." Something clicked in his brain, and he examined the picture of the short, skinny man a little closer. Earlier, they'd been a bit preoccupied with running for their lives. He hadn't had time to think about who these men might be.

"Smoke is coming out of your ears," said Bridget.

Bryan tapped the piece of paper. "Something about this guy is ringing a bell." He looked up from the paper. "Where is Sarah, anyway?"

"She's reading through her statement so she can sign it." Bridget poked him in the chest. "I'll need to do a sit-down with you, too."

He stared at the printout. "Can we do it later?"

"Sure, but I don't want to wait too long." She returned to her desk.

Bryan gripped the corners of the computer-generated photograph. The skinny thug was connected to a previous case he'd worked. That had to be why the guy looked familiar. He'd seen him in another photograph. His brain clicked through the possibilities. Only one case had been the focus of his attention since he'd come back to Discovery.

He peered around one of the carrels where a young officer with a buzz cut and thick eyebrows sat with a stack of papers in front of him.

Bryan waved the printout. "Grant, do you know what they did with my old case files?"

"They're right where you left them. You only took a leave of absence—no one was going to pack away your stuff."

Bryan worked his way to the back of the station. A six-foot-high divider separated the detectives' work area from the patrol officers' desks. His desk had been swept clean of anything personal, but it looked like someone had bothered to keep the dust from collecting. After retrieving his work phone from a drawer and placing it on the charger, he opened a file drawer and pulled out three thick manila files. How much surveillance and how many thousands of photographs had he taken?

He flipped open the first folder, shuffling through the photographs, and then the second as his heart pounded in his chest with anticipation. Was he so obsessed with Mason that he had imagined a connection? One after another, he looked at the photos and laid them aside.

Finally, he found the photograph he'd been looking for. Tyler Mason dressed in his usual expensive suit outside of a hotel in Mexico flanked by two men who were obviously acting as his bodyguards.

One of them was the same guy who had run his truck off the road.

Bryan swallowed. His fingers curled into a fist. If these guys were connected to Tyler Mason, this thing was way bigger than a couple of low-level drug dealers looking to get paid. Could this be the break he needed to blow the Mason case wide open?

"Keyes, I need to get your statement." Bridget's head peered around the divider, pulling him out of deep thought.

"Yes, of course. Is Sarah still in the interview room?"

"She was done. She said something about going to find her brother," Bridget said.

He let go of the photo as it drifted down to the desk. "She's out there by herself?" A sense of urgency girded his words.

Bridget shrugged. "She called a friend to come get her. What's the big deal?"

"I'm concerned those guys she tangled with aren't going to give up that easily."

"Don't you think they are still tromping through the woods or sitting in the back of a sheriff's car by now?"

"I'm pretty sure they have friends in town." His heart pounded from the sense of urgency he felt. "What was her home address?"

Bridget tilted her head. "I don't know if I can disclose that."

He grabbed her forearm. "You heard from the report how determined these guys were. I have a feeling they're not working alone."

Bridget let out a breath. "Okay. It was on Madison Street...." She thought for a moment and then looked down at the stack of papers she held in the crook of her elbow, flipping through several pages. "Three twenty-one Madison Street, that subdivision on the edge of town."

After grabbing his phone off the charger, he stalked toward the front of the station, his mind racing as he walked. His truck was floating down the Jefferson River. His car was parked at his house. He stopped in front of the young officer he'd talked to earlier. "Grant, loan me the keys to your car."

Grant raised his eyebrows. "Because…?"

"Because you're my friend and you can come out to my place and get them when you get off shift."

Maybe Grant picked up on the desperation in his voice, but he tossed the keys without further questions. "You owe me, buddy. I'm going to have to get a ride from my wife to go out there and get the car."

"Yeah, yeah. Thanks, man." Bryan pushed through the doors of the station and skirted around to the side parking lot where the officers kept their private cars.

His thoughts sparked at lightning speed as he sat behind the wheel and shoved the key in the ignition. It couldn't be just coincidence that the same man who worked for Tyler Mason had been after Sarah. Maybe he'd cut short his fire-tower hiatus and come back on the police force if Sandoval would let him pursue the connection.

He'd talk to the chief later. Right now he needed to make sure Sarah was not in any immediate danger.

SIX

"Thanks for the ride, Cindy." Sarah shut the passenger-side door of the compact car and made her way up her sidewalk.

Cindy leaned out of her open window. "You've been through a lot. Take a hot bath and try to forget about it. Don't worry about coming in to work tomorrow."

Cindy was not only her friend but also her supervisor at the adoption agency. Still, Sarah shook her head. "Work is the best thing for me. I'll be there tomorrow."

Cindy waved and sped off down the gravel road. Sarah crossed her arms. Though it was past dinner time, the sky was still a cloudless blue. At this point in the summer, it didn't get dark until nine o'clock. The temperatures had soared to the high nineties in the middle of the day and were only just starting to drop. Still, between her river-drenched clothes and the edge of fear she couldn't shake, Sarah was shivering. It was past time to get inside where she could get warm, and maybe start to feel safe again.

Sarah turned back toward her house. She lived on the edge of town on a two-acre plot. Her nearest neighbor was not visible around a bend in the road. Across the road, there was only a cornfield.

A chill ran down her back when she saw her purse and tote lying on the grass. She'd dropped them when the kidnappers grabbed her. She placed her palm on her chest where her heart pounded erratically with fear. Was she even safe here anymore? Would they come back for her? Or would they give up now that it was clear she didn't have the information they wanted? Probably not. Though finding her brother seemed to be their priority, eliminating her was now a concern, as well. She was a loose end. She knew what they looked like.

Sarah gathered up her purse and tote. Her cell phone had fallen out. She picked it up and put it in her jacket pocket. She retrieved her extra set of keys from the hide-a-key. After putting her keys in her pocket as well, she turned the doorknob and stepped inside. Shadows shrouded the living room in gray light. She'd drawn the shades to keep the place cool during the day.

The house was completely silent. She couldn't recall if she had let her cat, Mr. Tiddlywinks, out before when she'd come home for lunch. She took in a sharp breath as anxiety threaded through her chest. Maybe it was a mistake to come home.

Had the sheriff caught up with the men in the forest or had they found a way back into town? Even if the sheriff didn't catch them, it would take them hours to walk to a road where they could hitch a ride. She had some time to come up with a plan. She could stay with Cindy for a while, but she didn't want to bring danger to her friend.

Her thoughts turned to Bryan. She wouldn't have to worry about his safety—he could clearly take care of himself. She'd been anxious to leave the station without saying goodbye to him. Dormant feelings of hurt and confusion came alive in his presence. Still, she felt the assurance of protection when she was around him. Part of her wished she hadn't been so hasty in leaving.

The rest of her realized that there was no time to waste. She was exhausted and bruised. Cindy's suggestion of a nice hot bath sounded wonderful, but she knew she couldn't. Finding Crew was her priority. The window she had to warn Crew before those men found their way back to town could be closing.

Sarah retrieved a comb from the bathroom and got the glass out of her hair. She set out a change of clothes.

Her stomach growled. She needed to eat something quick. Sarah walked over to the refrigerator and pulled out a yogurt. While she ate, she'd come up with a strategy for locating Crew.

Discovery was only a town of about fifty thousand people, but locating a homeless person was never easy. Still, she knew some of their hangouts. She'd start with the shelter where her friend Julia worked.

A squeaking sound alerted her to a fat yellow cat running his paws up and down the glass of the patio door. "Mr. Tiddlywinks. Did you miss me?" She slid the glass door open, allowing the cat to meander in. He rubbed against her leg. She lifted up the fat cat who weighed at least ten pounds. He purred in her arms.

The silence of her house unnerved her. Logically, she knew those men couldn't come after her so quickly. Still, she couldn't shake the fear that embedded itself in every muscle in her body. She shuddered as images of the kidnapping washed over her like a wall of water. Only the memory of Bryan's steady voice, of his hand grabbing hers calmed her.

Sarah sat the cat back down on the floor. She reached over and rested her hand on the countertop for support. While the cat ate his food, she checked to make sure the patio door was locked.

She took her yogurt and stood in the living room staring out across the road at the ditch and the open field beyond that. A car rolled slowly past, crunching gravel beneath its tires. The hair on the back of Sarah's neck electrified. That wasn't one of her neighbors' cars.

She turned back toward the kitchen. A man wearing a mask stood at the patio door, raising the butt of a rifle to smash it against the glass.

Dropping her yogurt, Sarah turned and flung open the front door. The car that had gone by moments before was turned around and waiting ten yards away.

Sarah turned and sprinted up the road. The car rumbled toward her. The masked man with the rifle came around the side of the house. The car drew closer. She struggled for breath, willing her legs to pump. The rumble of the car engine surrounded her.

She dove into the ditch. If she cut across the field, there was a house on the other side. But she had to get there first. And now, in addition to the attacker with the rifle, the man in the car had gotten out and was chasing her.

Sarah stumbled and fell. She rolled over on her back. The man from the car was the first to close the distance between them. He dropped to his knees and grabbed her. She screamed, kicking and flailing her arms. She tore off his ski mask. Car Man was a stranger—he definitely wasn't Deep Voice or Acne Scars. *How many of them are there?* she wondered. *How many will come after me?*

She managed a blow to his nose, and he reeled backward. She crawled through the tall grass. He grabbed her ankle and yanked her backward. Rocks and hard dirt grazed her stomach.

She rolled over on her back, kicking, trying to break free. He lunged toward her, squeezing her biceps and shaking her. "You're coming with me." He was all teeth and bloodshot eyes. His fingers tightened around her arms.

Footsteps pounded. She saw an elbow and an arm suction around the man's neck. He was jerked backward, his eyes wild with surprise.

The man let go of Sarah. She fell to the ground and scrambled away, eyes wide as she looked at…

Bryan!

He had Car Man in a choke hold that he didn't release until the man had gone still. He let go, and the man fell to the ground, not moving. Bryan glanced toward the road where Rifle Man still jogged toward them.

He reached out for Sarah's hand. "This way."

He pulled her toward the field of corn.

Sarah glanced over her shoulder. Rifle Man was taking aim. A red dot appeared on Bryan's shoulder blade. Sarah pushed Bryan to the ground.

"What're you doing?" Bryan protested.

She gestured to where the red laser dot was now skimming over the grass.

She caught the look of stunned gratitude on Bryan's face. They crawled the short distance to the high corn ready for harvest.

A rifle shot zinged through the air, slicing a cornstalk above them. Bryan angled sideways, altering the direction he crawled but still moving toward the shelter of the corn. Sarah scrambled behind him. Once shielded by the rows of corn, they half crouched, half ran.

Another rifle shot popped behind them.

Bryan grabbed her hand. "My car is a ways from your house. I saw what was going on and jumped out. If we can get to it, we can escape."

He parted the stalks of corn. Crouching low, they moved perpendicular to the rows. He stopped, turned toward her and placed a finger over his lips.

Sarah held her breath and listened. She detected a swishing sound. One of the men was moving through the cornfield.

Bryan lifted his head above the corn and then dove back down. He pulled on Sarah's sleeve. They wove through the rows, zigzagging and backtracking to try to throw off their pursuer. Again, Bryan tilted his head to get a read on where the man was. Wind rushed over the top of the corn.

A rifle shot hit right in front of them. Sarah stifled a scream but her heart pounded so hard she thought it would break her rib cage. Bryan grabbed her hand and pulled her along the furrows between rows. They ran as fast as they could while still bending at the waist until they came to the edge of the field.

Both of them lay on their stomachs while Bryan separated the stalks so they could look out. Her house was about a quarter mile up the road. She could see the assailants' car and Car Man not far from her house. He patrolled up and down the road, watching the cornfield. Midway between the cornfield and her house was Bryan's car, parked at an angle on the gravel road with the driver's-side door flung open.

Bryan whispered in her ear. "We'll use the ditch for shelter and then swing around the side of the car so they don't notice us until the last second."

Sarah nodded. They waited for the moment when the guard on the road turned his back and then slipped out of the cornfield and crawled up the ditch, soldier-style. Once they were close to the car, they waited until Car Man turned his back again before racing to the back bumper and around to the passenger-side door. Bryan crawled in first and slipped over to the driver's seat. He slid down low in the seat to avoid detection.

Sarah crawled in, leaning forward—careful not to be seen above the dashboard.

Bryan's face went pale. His mouth hung open.

Panic spread through her like wildfire. "What?"

Still crouched low in the seat, he padded his pockets and then touched the steering wheel. "They took the keys."

Sarah's throat went dry as a shiver ran down her back.

She lifted her head a few inches above the dashboard. Car Man had spotted them and was now making a bee-line for them.

"He's seen us."

Bryan reached under the dash. "Old car like this. I can hot-wire it."

Rifle Man raced toward them from the cornfield as well, holding his rifle with both hands.

Bryan sorted through the wires he had pulled out.

They were sitting ducks—and both assailants were closing in. "Hurry." Fear paralyzed Sarah.

The car sparked to life. Bryan reached over and closed the driver's-side door while shifting out of Park.

"Stay down." Bryan pressed his hand softly on her head. He hit the gas and sped toward Car Man.

Bryan's arm rested over her back as she leaned forward, the warmth of his touch seeping through her cotton shirt. She lifted her head just above the dashboard. They whizzed past the man on the road.

Sarah looked out the back window as Bryan gained speed, creating a dust cloud behind them. Both men ran for their car. Her house grew smaller as they sped away.

One thing was clear. She wouldn't be able to stay in her own home until they found Crew and got to the bottom of this.

The assailants' car gained on them.

Bryan gripped the steering wheel. "What's the fastest way back to civilization from here?"

Sarah glanced out the side windows and then through the windshield trying to get her bearings. "Take a left at the next crossroads."

"If we can get into some traffic, they're not likely to try to come at us." Bryan leaned forward, hyperfocused on the landscape in front of him.

The pursuers' car was within twenty feet of them.

They drew close to the crossroads. The other car edged toward their back bumper. Bryan pressed harder on the gas.

Sarah dug her fingers into the dashboard. "Not too fast. The gravel acts like marbles and you'll flip the car."

Every muscle in Bryan's arm tensed as he spoke through clenched teeth. "We're all right."

He stared straight ahead, his gaze locked in place until he made an abrupt left turn at the crossroads, not slowing down and spitting gravel with his back tires. Sarah pressed her back against the seat and dug into the armrest as the back end of the car lifted into the air.

The car landed on the paved road with a bump. Bryan pressed the accelerator to the floor.

The pursuers' car overshot the turn and veered over to the other side of the road, fishtailing.

The distance between the two cars lengthened. Several cars going in the opposite direction whizzed past them.

Sarah took in a breath. "The highway that leads back into town intersects with this road. We'll be there in a few minutes."

Bryan sat back in his seat, relaxing his grip on the wheel. "Good. Do you have a friend you can stay with?"

"Yes, but that's not where I want to go right away. I need to find Crew. I have to warn him and find out what this is all about and get him to a safe place, too."

Bryan glanced over at her. "Let's get the police to take care of that. I'll help them."

"He's my brother. This is my problem," Sarah said.

Bryan approached the stop sign where the country road intersected with the multilane highway. "Does your friend know how to use a gun or have a husband who does?"

Sarah looked behind her. The other car was gaining on them again. "You're not hearing me. I'm not going to my friend's house until I find Crew. He's my brother. I will deal with this."

"Those thugs couldn't find your brother. What makes you think you can?"

"My determination." She didn't want to have to take any more help from Bryan.

"They seem pretty determined to me. You're not safe, Sarah. Do you understand that?"

"I can handle this."

He pulled out onto the highway. "Look, I don't know exactly what is going on here, but this is way bigger than Crew owing a couple of low-level dealers money. Whoever is behind this has resources. You've had two sets of thugs come after you."

Sarah laced her fingers together and bit her lip. Bryan was right. They knew where she lived. They might even know where she worked and who her friends were.

"The only way to end this is to find Crew. I'm going to start by asking around at the homeless shelter. I have a friend who works there."

Bryan let out an exasperated sigh. "Then I'm coming with you."

"Fine, if that is what you want to do." Her tone was defiant, but Sarah found herself secretly grateful for his help and protection, however stirred up he made her feel.

They came to the mall on the edge of town. "Where is this homeless shelter anyway?"

"On Division Street. I guess a lot of this is new since you were last here."

Bryan nodded. "I've only been back for five months."

She took in a breath, trying to calm down. "What made you come back here?"

"An investigation I had been working on in Spokane for more than a year. Turns out Discovery is ground zero for the whole operation." Bryan slowed down as they entered the heart of town.

"Oh." So it was his work that had brought him back

here. She couldn't hide her disappointment. Why had she even hoped that he'd come back to see her?

"The last I heard of you, you had left for college. I assumed you were never coming back," he said.

Her spirits lifted. "You kept tabs on me?"

"I stayed in touch with some of the people even if I didn't come back," he said.

"When I left, I didn't intend to come back. But then, Crew was here and my adoptive parents were here." She turned to look at him. "I guess Discovery will always be home for me."

He held her in his gaze for a long moment. She thought she saw affection in his eyes. What was running through his head? Did Discovery only hold bad memories for him?

The evening sky turned gray as they approached the dead-end street where the homeless shelter was. Sarah checked her watch. They had maybe an hour of daylight left.

Once it turned dark, the chances of finding Crew would be close to zero. The homeless shelter came into view.

Sarah craned her neck to look out the back window. How long did they have before this new group of men caught up with them?

SEVEN

Bryan glanced in his rearview mirror. Nobody was behind them, yet he couldn't shake the feeling of being watched. He parked the car beside the shelter and looked over at Sarah. She still had the same clothes that had gotten soaked in the river earlier. The ruffled button-down shirt she wore might have been white at some point but he doubted it ever would be again. He hadn't changed either since getting back to town. His T-shirt was ripped, his worn jeans sported mud stains and he had bruises on his arms. "We look like homeless people."

Sarah laughed, a soft, easy laugh that had always been music to his ears. "We'll blend right in."

As they approached the shelter, they saw two men seated on the steps while a third used a bucket as a chair. One of the men on the steps stared at the ground and hugged himself, but the other man met Bryan's gaze.

Sarah stepped forward. "I'm looking for Crew Langston. Have you guys seen him?"

The man who refused to make eye contact shot up abruptly from the steps and wandered away, shuffling his feet.

The man on the bucket squinted and tilted his head toward the darkening sky. "Crew Langston?"

Sarah directed her comment toward the man on the

bucket. "He's a tall, thin guy with dark hair. Likes to wear denim shirts and a bandanna around his neck."

The man on the steps let out a heavy breath and said, "I don't know the guy."

"I heard he got clean and got himself a place on Sixteenth Street." The man on the bucket touched his matted gray hair.

"I didn't hear anything like that," the man on the steps replied.

"You don't even know the guy."

The other man lifted his chin in the air and crossed his arms. "I know his name...."

The two men had descended into one of the illogical discussions common to people with mental illness. They probably weren't going to get any more information out of them. Could they trust the information they'd been given?

Although he doubted he'd get much of an answer, Bryan gave it one more try. "Do you know the address on Sixteenth Street where Crew is living? Or even what the house looks like?"

The man on the bucket shook his head. "Didn't see it for myself. Just what I heard."

"You ask too many questions," said the man on the steps, cutting a suspicious glance toward Bryan. He closed his eyes and turned his head, indicating that the conversation was over.

Bryan tugged on Sarah's shirt so she stepped away from the two men. "Sixteenth Street runs most of the length of town."

Sarah crossed her arms and stared up at the sky. "That would be wonderful though if my brother had a place of his own. If it's true." Her voice held a note of hope. "It'll be dark soon. I suppose we could drive up and down the street and hope we see him."

Bryan pulled out his cell phone. "There has to be a

faster way." Who did he know who could connect him to that kind of information? "Even if Crew does have a place, I doubt he's staying there right now. I'm sure word has gotten to him that those thugs are looking for him."

"They might not know Crew has a place. It was news to me and I'm his sister."

She could be right. His training as a detective told him to follow whatever lead, no matter how thin. "Give me a minute to make some calls." He'd start with one of the officers whose patrol took him on that street.

"I'm going inside to talk with my friend Julia. She might know something." Sarah trotted up the stairs and disappeared.

Sarah's voice floated out from an open window. He felt a tug at his heart when he heard her ask a question and then laugh. He had to admit that he still cared for her after all this time, but after the way he'd been so immature and let her down all those years ago, she'd probably want nothing to do with him once they found Crew. Sarah's voice faded and Bryan turned his attention to figuring out where Crew might be living.

After talking to a couple of officers, Bryan managed to narrow a probable location down to a two-block area where someone matching Crew's description had been seen in the last few weeks. It was something, anyway. He glanced up from his phone at the warm glow coming from the homeless shelter. Maybe Sarah had had better luck.

"Hey, Sarah."

Sarah looked up in the direction of the voice. A man dressed in a long coat and knit hat offered her a gap-toothed grin.

She couldn't find Julia in the shelter and had wandered out the back door to see if anyone else knew anything about Crew.

She turned toward the man who called her name.

"Eddie?" Eddie was one of Crew's friends. They'd eaten lunch together months ago when Crew called her and asked if they could meet. Eddie was not an addict, but a man prone to wandering when he went off his schizophrenia medication. Though he looked closer to forty, Eddie was in his mid-twenties. His parents, an older couple, had gotten used to a pattern of their son coming in and out of their lives. They supplied Eddie with a cell phone so he could call them when he wanted to come home.

From the light she saw in his eyes, she was catching him on a good day.

Eddie edged toward her. "I heard you asking around. You're looking for Crew?"

She nodded as hope fluttered in her heart. "Do you know where he is?"

"I saw him less than half an hour ago. I can take you to him. It's just over by the fairgrounds."

Sarah turned in the direction Eddie indicated. The high chain-link fence and labyrinth of buildings that made up the fairgrounds were visible from the homeless shelter. Because the buildings were underutilized, the fairgrounds were a known hangout for homeless people when events weren't being held there.

"Can I get my friend to come with us?" She pointed in the general direction Bryan might be.

"No, only you. That guy's a cop. I can tell." He sounded afraid. "We should hurry. Some guys were after Crew. He might not be there much longer."

Sarah steeled herself. Eddie had huge trust issues. It wasn't really surprising that Bryan made him nervous. She didn't want to scare him away. She had to find Crew. "You'll stay with me, Eddie?"

Eddie looked at the ground, shifted his weight. "It's not far."

He led her through an opening in the fence that surrounded the fairgrounds, past several buildings and corrals. Four homeless people huddled in a tight circle craned their necks as Sarah and Eddie passed by.

"In here." Eddie pushed open a door that had a broken padlock. They stepped inside a long, narrow exhibit building. Sarah squinted. The building had a series of low-walled stalls where kids showed their 4-H animals. Shadows covered most of the building.

"Where is he?"

A tiny light came on at the other end of the building.

"Crew?" Sarah walked toward the light. She heard a scuffling sound behind her and when she turned back around, she saw that Eddie had disappeared.

Sensing danger, Sarah stopped. Had Eddie been spooked? Was that why he'd left her behind? A man at the other end of the building stalked toward her. She squinted. "Crew, is that you?"

"Sarah Langston." The man came closer, holding a flashlight. He was dressed in a suit. As he drew near, she saw that he was clean-shaven. "I have a message for you."

"Is it from my brother?"

In the distance, she heard Bryan shouting her name. His voice grew louder.

The man seemed on edge, glancing from side to side.

"Please tell me. What is the message?"

"Sarah." Bryan stood in the doorway.

When Sarah spun back around, the man was gone.

Bryan approached her. "What were you doing here?"

"There was a man who might know something about my brother."

"A homeless man?"

"No—well, yes and no. The man who was waiting here for me wasn't homeless. He was wearing a suit. But it was one of Crew's friends who led me here." Sarah tried to sort through what had just happened. "He lied to me." Eddie must have been paid to be the courier and bring her to the other man. That's why he'd claimed to have seen Crew. He knew she wouldn't come unless she thought she'd be meeting her brother.

"What did the man say?"

"You scared him away." Sarah walked the length of the dark building with Bryan following her. "He said he had a message for me."

"He didn't say specifically he had a message about Crew?"

"No, but what else would it be about?" She stood beside the half-open door the man must have slipped out of. She stepped outside into the darkness. The man had clearly been nervous and was probably long gone by now. Eddie would be much easier to track down. "We have to find Eddie. He must know something."

They searched the fairgrounds, the shelter and an area by the river where homeless people often slept. No sign of Eddie.

Bryan placed a supportive hand on Sarah's shoulder as they headed back toward the car. "I've narrowed down the possibilities for where Crew's place might be. Let's go see if we can find it before we call it a night."

Bryan's car rolled slowly down Sixteenth Street. Most of the houses looked like single-family dwellings. Nothing Crew could afford even with assistance.

"There, maybe." Sarah pointed to a three-story building that had a number of apartment units. A man stood outside, tossing a garbage bag into a Dumpster. Sarah jumped out of the car and approached the man who looked to be about college-age.

"I'm looking for someone." She pulled out her phone and clicked through her photos until she found a picture of Crew. "This man."

The young man looked at the photograph. "Yeah, I've seen that guy."

Sarah's spirits lifted. "Really?"

"I've talked to him when he was on his way home from work. He lives in the basement apartment over there." The man pointed across the street. "Haven't seen him around for a couple of days, but he's got a roommate."

"Thank you." Sarah headed across the street.

They descended a concrete stairway and Sarah tapped on the door. "I know he's not going to be here. But maybe the roommate knows something."

"It's a place to start." Bryan sounded encouraged, too.

They waited. Sarah rocked heel to toe. "It's kind of late. Do you think the roommate is sleeping?"

Bryan leaned forward and tapped on the door a second time—louder this time. "The clock is ticking for your brother. We can get somebody out of bed if we have to."

Sarah smiled. Glad she didn't have to do this alone even though it was Bryan who was helping her.

They heard footsteps and then the door swung open to reveal a man dressed in a brown uniform. He was a few years younger than Crew, clean-shaven with a narrow face and thin nose.

"We're sorry to bother you so late at night," Sarah said.

The man shrugged. "Actually, I was just getting ready for work. Graveyard shift, security."

Bryan leaned in the doorway. "We wanted to talk to you about your roommate, Crew Langston."

"Crew hasn't been around for like three days. Which is really weird because the guy has been hyperresponsible since he got clean."

"I'm his sister. Do you know where he might have gone?"

The young man's face brightened. "You're Sarah? Why don't you come in?" He stood to one side so they could enter. "I'm Nick Sheridan, by the way."

They stepped inside. The apartment was clean and sparse.

"Like I said, I don't know where he's gone. They called from his work. He didn't show up for his shift there. That old beater car he bought is gone, too."

So Crew had saved enough to buy a car. How long had he been clean? Why hadn't he told her? "You have no idea where he went? He didn't say anything to you?" Sarah fought off a rising sense of desperation as she struggled to find the right question to ask.

Nick shook his head.

She asked the question she was dreading the answer to. "Do you think he started using drugs again?"

"He was pretty serious about his recovery. He wanted to give it a full six months before he told you to make sure he was going to make it this time."

"He said that?" Sarah's throat went tight from joy. Tears formed at the corner of her eyes.

"Yeah, your opinion of him means a lot to him." Nick buttoned up the shirt of his uniform. "If you don't mind, I'll be late for work if I don't get going."

"Oh, sorry." They still didn't have any information that would give them a clue as to why Crew would disappear or why the men were after him.

The man picked up his keys and headed toward the door.

Bryan spoke up. "Was there anything unusual in the days before he left?"

Bryan's question seemed to spark something. "Come to think of it, a blonde woman came to see him about a week ago. She wasn't someone I had ever seen him with before." The man moved toward the door and Sarah and Bryan followed him.

"Do you know what they talked about?"

He stepped outside. "They went for a walk. When she arrived, she seemed upset or scared." He shrugged. "I only saw her that one time. Crew disappeared a few days after that." He placed his key in the door and locked it.

Bryan pulled a card from his wallet. "Let us know if you hear anything more from him or remember anything else."

Sarah dug through her pockets for a card of her own. "I really need to talk to my brother."

The man examined both cards. "Sure, I'll let you know if I hear anything."

They stepped up into the dark night and headed toward the car. Sarah slipped into the passenger seat and the heaviness of fatigue set in.

"So tell me where your friend lives and I'll drop you off," Bryan said.

Sarah gave him directions to Cindy's house. "And for your information, she does have a husband, but I have no idea if he owns a gun."

"She lives in town?"

Sarah nodded.

Bryan cruised through the quiet residential streets. A warm glow came from some of the house windows. Others were dark.

Sarah's life had flipped completely upside-down from where she had been this afternoon when she thought she would leave her house after lunch and finish a day of work. She'd found out that her brother had gotten his life together and had fallen off the face of the earth all in a few short hours. And now Bryan was back in her life. She wasn't sure how she felt about that. His police training was invaluable and had already saved her life. For that, she was grateful. Dormant feelings of attraction had been stirred up by his return. But every time she thought about how he had abandoned her when she'd needed him most, a shield went over her heart.

Thinking about what Bryan meant to her after all these

years would make her fall apart. She preferred to focus her energy on finding Crew.

She voiced the thought that teased the corners of her mind. "If it's not drugs or a debt, what is it? What's happened to my brother?"

Bryan shook his head. "Hard to say. I wonder who this woman is who came to his place…if she's the reason he's gone underground."

"I doubt he had much money. He couldn't get far." Sarah felt a rising frustration at the lack of answers. She watched the houses clip by through the subdivision. "That's it. Cindy's house is on the cul-de-sac."

Bryan slowed and checked his rearview mirror. He sat up a little straighter. "Is there another friend you might want to stay with?"

Sarah looked around. "Why?"

Bryan looped around the cul-de-sac past Cindy's house. He turned back out onto the street. A moment later, he tilted his head back. "That's why."

Through the back window, Sarah saw a car pull away from the curb and slip in behind them. Anxiety coiled through her. Not again. "They aren't going to give up, are they?"

"I thought maybe they were just headed in the same direction as us. But when they pulled in at the edge of the cul-de-sac and didn't get out to go into a house, I knew something was up."

"How did they find us?" Weariness and fear wrestled within her.

"They probably had Crew's place staked out."

The car hung about twenty feet behind them. They weren't exactly being stealthy.

"Now they're trying to intimidate us." Sarah's voice held a tremble.

Bryan adjusted his hands on the steering wheel. His

voice remained steady. "Or they are just waiting for an opportunity."

Sarah wiggled in her seat. "So what do we do?"

"I can't just dump you at a friend's house."

"I agree. That would put them in danger, too."

"We'll stay close to civilization, try and shake them off. They're not going to try anything if there's a risk of being caught."

"Where do we find civilization at this hour?"

Bryan sped up. "I'll think of something."

Sarah turned around again. The menacing glow of the headlights behind them fed her fear.

EIGHT

Bryan drove through town. They needed to hole up somewhere for a while. So many of the businesses were new to him—and he was sure that a lot of the places he remembered had closed over the years he'd been gone. "Is Martin's still open twenty-four hours?"

"I think so." Her voice sounded strained.

He pushed toward the edge of town and up a hill. When he checked the rearview mirror, there was no one behind them. But he knew that didn't mean they were in the clear.

These guys had to be working for Mason. They were organized and professional, which would make them very hard to shake. But if he could *prove* the connection to Mason, then this could be the link he needed. His instinct told him that this could reopen the case he wanted so badly to see brought to trial, but what he needed was more evidence, a tighter connection than a thug who had been photographed with Mason and had come after Sarah.

Martin's was an all-night diner and truck stop best known for its milk shakes. Bryan pulled into the lot, relieved to see it was still open. Several semitrucks were parked in the far corner of the lot. Inside, three patrons hunched over their food in booths. All three were men, all three sat by themselves.

Bryan studied the décor...or lack of it. "This place brings back some memories."

They had had more than one date here. Sometimes after football games, half the school would come here to celebrate or commiserate.

"Yeah…some memories." Sarah's voice laced with pain.

"Sorry, maybe it wasn't the best choice," Bryan said.

"No, it's one of the few places that are open at this hour…and ten years is a long time, right? We should be over it by now."

He stared at her for a long moment, wondering what she meant. Over the pain they had caused each other? Or over the love they had felt?

A fifty-something waitress with candy-apple red hair and purple eye shadow set two menus on the table. "Still got a pot of coffee going. Grill's been closed down for an hour. I can do sandwiches or reheat some lasagna."

"Actually, just a pot of tea and maybe a couple of slices of that blueberry pie I saw on the way in," Bryan said.

Sarah settled in the booth opposite Bryan. A soft smile graced her lips. "You remembered blueberry was my favorite."

The waitress brought the tea and pie. Bryan sipped his tea and watched Sarah dig into her pie. He liked the way she closed her eyes after each bite, relishing the sweetness and flavor. Her curly brown hair fell in layers around her face and her cheeks had a natural glow. She'd always had a prettiness that was unassuming, not created from makeup and endless beauty routines.

She wiped a dab of blueberry from her lips and smiled at him. Her gaze shifted over his shoulder and her smile faded away. She laid her fork on the table and continued to stare.

"That's him."

Bryan craned his neck to see what she was looking at—a television screen running a local commercial for a used car dealership.

She pointed to the man on the screen who called himself Crazy Ray. "That's the guy I saw in that building Eddie led me to."

"Are you sure?"

Sarah slipped out of the booth and walked closer to the television, nodding her head. "That's him. I'm sure of it." She turned and sat back down in the booth.

Bryan shook his head. This didn't make any sense. There was a part of him that thought maybe the well-dressed guy at the fairgrounds had been Mason. Was he so desperate to nail Mason that he was trying to make connections that didn't exist?

Sarah poured another cup of tea. She took several sips and then yawned. "I'm really tired. I want to sleep in my own bed."

"It's just not safe to do that, Sarah."

She rolled her eyes. "I know that's how it has to be. I don't have to like it, though."

He thought for a moment. "The female officer you spoke to, Bridget, gets off duty in an hour or so. You'd be safe with her. We can call her, see if that will work."

Sarah rested her head against the back of the booth. "Okay, if that's what we have to do...." She closed her eyes. "I drank a lot of tea. I need to use the little girls' room."

"I'll call Bridget." Bryan pulled out his phone.

Sarah rose from her seat and walked toward the counter where the waitress was filling salt and pepper shakers. The waitress pointed off to one side and Sarah disappeared around a corner.

Bryan phoned Bridget. Once he explained the situation, she was glad to take Sarah in for the night.

"I've approached Sandoval about protection already, but that was before the attack at her house. Maybe he'll reconsider," Bryan said.

He talked for a few minutes more before hanging up

and then he called Sandoval to let him know there was no need to do a patrol past Sarah's house, since she wouldn't be there. Sandoval said he'd look into what he could do for protection for Sarah now that there was clearly an ongoing threat. Bryan said goodbye and hung up.

One of the truckers got up and lumbered toward the door. Bryan watched the corner where Sarah had turned. She should have been back by now.

He rose to his feet and headed in the direction Sarah had gone. Around the corner, he found a room that had probably been a casino or bar at one time but now was empty. He spotted the restroom and walked over to it.

"Sarah?" He knocked. "Sarah." He scanned the room. His gaze rested on a glass door in the corner. Panic sparked inside of him. The thugs could have been watching through the windows, waiting for their chance, and grabbed Sarah when she headed to the restroom. He ran toward the door and flung it open, searching the dark landscape. The lights of downtown Discovery glowed two blocks away.

He ran outside, feet crunching the asphalt.

Then he heard a scream. He sprinted in the direction of the sound. He turned a corner to see lights on a pickup truck come on. The truck moved slowly through the lot. That had to be the one.

He stayed in the shadows for a moment and then sprinted toward the truck. He jumped into the truck bed just as it accelerated through the lot. There was a passenger in the cab. It had to be Sarah.

She turned her head slightly, eyes growing wide. Her mouth had duct tape over it. Bryan scanned the truck bed for a weapon. He picked up a jack, leaned out the side of the bed and smashed it against the driver's-side window.

The car swerved wildly, crossing the center line. A horn blared. Bryan tried to hold on and brace himself, but there was no time. The truck smashed into an oncoming car.

Bryan flew backward. His body impacted with a hard object. He heard screaming just as he lost consciousness.

Sarah pressed her back against the truck door, trying not to hyperventilate. She hadn't been injured in the crash, but she'd seen Bryan go flying. Was he all right? Was he even still alive? There was no way to know.

Her kidnapper had glass in his hair and blood streamed down his face from various cuts, but he was still conscious. "You stay here. You don't move, do you hear me?" He leaned toward her, poking a meaty finger in her chest. His eyes were wild with rage.

Sarah nodded, wishing she could push him away, but her hands were bound together in front of her with duct tape.

Though it was dark, a single working headlight on the other car revealed that the man behind the wheel of the other car was slumped forward. She craned her neck. Bryan had been thrown clear of the truck close to the edge of the road.

Her kidnapper walked over to the other car and peered inside. Satisfied that the other driver wasn't going to move, he skirted around the back of the truck and headed toward where Bryan lay facedown.

Sarah twisted at the waist and fumbled with the door handle. How far could she get running with her hands tied in front of her? She wouldn't have a chance to find out if she couldn't get the door unlocked.

She prayed for another car to come along. Her hand pressed against the door lock and got it released. Now for the handle. But before she could tackle that, the thug rolled Bryan down the bank out of view and returned to the truck.

He came to the driver's side, got in and turned the key. The engine chugalugged but didn't turn over. He tried several more times. He grimaced. He beat the dashboard with his fist.

Sarah recoiled at his anger. All she had to do was push the door open. Downtown Discovery was only a few blocks away. Martin's was just up the hill. If she got away, she could get help—send someone to Bryan to make sure he was all right. Someone would see her. If someone was out at this hour and if the kidnapper didn't catch her first.

The thug took out his phone and dialed. He waited for a moment and then spoke in a rapid-fire manner. "Listen, I'm outside Discovery just past Martin's. You better get over here quick. I got the package, but I'm in a world of hurt. Hurry."

He looked over at Sarah. "Get away from that door." He leaned forward and yanked on her shirt.

Sarah struggled to clear her head. This man hadn't killed her on the spot. Just like before, he must have intended to take her somewhere remote before killing her. The choice bought her a chance at escape, but how would she get away?

The thug leaned toward her. "Don't even think about running."

Sarah froze, knowing that now he'd be watching her like a hawk. But with his eyes on her, he didn't see the figure approaching the truck....

Bryan appeared in the driver's-side window with the jack in his hand. He hit the assailant on the back of the head. The beefy man slumped into Sarah's lap. She scooted toward the door. Bryan ran around the front of the truck, opened the passenger-side door and pulled Sarah out.

She turned to face him.

He touched the duct tape on her mouth. "One swift movement. It's gonna hurt."

She nodded.

He yanked. Her face stung. She sucked in air.

"He has help coming," she said.

Bryan pulled a pocketknife out of his jeans pocket and cut the duct tape on her hands. "Let's get going then." He glanced over at the other driver. "We can phone for help as soon as we're in the clear."

He pulled her away from the road into the darkness of the tangled brush. They headed up the hill toward Martin's and their car. Another truck whizzed by on the road, stopping at the accident, probably the kidnapper's backup.

Their feet pounded the hard earth until they came to the edge of Martin's parking lot where the lights didn't reach. They hid behind a line of Dumpsters. Bryan peered out. A man stood beside their car scanning the parking lot.

Sarah leaned close to him. "What is it?"

He watched the man a moment longer. "Could just be a guy waiting for a ride, but it's too risky. We can't go back to the car."

Bryan sat down beside her and pulled out his phone. "This is Bryan Keyes. There's an accident on the west end of town. Send an ambulance. We're being pursued. We need to be picked up. We're headed toward downtown."

Headlights shone toward the Dumpsters. Tires rolled slowly over asphalt.

"They found us." Fear saturated her voice as she grabbed his arm.

Bryan tugged on her sleeve. She followed him farther into the darkness. The land beside Martin's was a fenced field. Two empty city lots separated them from downtown. Behind them, the truck had stopped by the Dumpsters. Doors slammed.

Sirens sounded in the distance. "There's our ride," said Bryan. "Hopefully that will scare them away."

The two men came toward the field. Bryan stretched the barbed wire fence so Sarah could crawl through.

"Stay low," Bryan whispered. They sprinted toward a

clump of trees. The men came to the edge of the fence. One muttered something about a flashlight.

Two horses lying on the ground by the trees stirred to life as they approached. The sirens grew louder.

The horses whinnied and stomped. Sarah pressed close to one of them, so in the shadows it would look like she was part of the horse.

Light flashed across the field.

"Get on," said Bryan. "I'll boost you." He held his cupped hand toward her. Ride bareback? She hadn't done it in years. But Bryan wasn't giving her much of a choice as he hoisted her up onto the horse's back. "Ride to the edge of the field. Work your way toward downtown."

She didn't have time to ask him what he was going to do before he slapped the horse's flank. Sarah pressed against the horse's back and held on to its mane. Behind her, the flashlight bobbed up and down as the men raced across the field.

The horse's hooves pounded out a rhythm against the soft ground. A second set of hooves thundered behind her. She could just make out Bryan's silhouette. When her own horse came to an abrupt stop, Sarah slipped off and made her way toward the fence. Bryan was right behind her.

The flashlight no longer bobbed across the field.

Bryan leaned close to her and whispered, "It'll take them a minute to regroup."

They crawled through the fence and entered a residential part of town. Most of the houses were dark. From inside one of them a dog barked as they ran past. Lights came on.

Their escape through the field had caused them to veer away from downtown. Main Street was at least four blocks away. An ambulance went by. They slowed their pace, though Bryan continued to glance around.

The glow of the downtown lights came into view. A

police car with its light flashing was parked in a parking lot. The officer got out as they approached.

"I was afraid you weren't going to make our date," the officer joked.

"We got a little hung up." Bryan slapped the other officer on the shoulder blade. "Sarah, this is Grant."

Sarah nodded.

Compassion colored Grant's features. They must look like they'd been put through the wringer. "Are you sure you don't want to go to the emergency room?"

"We need to get her to the station. I'm convinced that it's the only place she'll be safe right now."

Bryan opened the passenger-side door of the patrol car. "The back is kind of uncomfortable. I'll ride back there."

Sarah slipped into the front passenger seat. The officer's computer took up a lot of the seat space. Grant got behind the wheel and swung the car around.

"Oh, by the way." Bryan leaned forward. "Your car's parked up by Martin's."

"Thanks a lot, buddy," Grant said.

Bryan was probably joking around to forget about what they had just been through, but the camaraderie between the two men did nothing to lighten Sarah's spirits.

She rested her head against the seat. She rubbed her wrists where the duct tape had been. She touched the bandage on her forehead. Though she made no noise, tears formed at the corners of her eyes and flowed down her cheeks. She stared, not really seeing the view in front of her. Would this ever come to an end?

From behind, a gentle, warm hand touched her shoulder and squeezed.

NINE

Bryan flipped through the Mason file for the umpteenth time. At least when he had been up in the fire tower, he'd been able to think of something other than this case. But here at the station, it seemed to meet him at every turn.

He checked his watch. It was nearly noon. Sarah had fallen asleep on a couch in the break room after freshening up in the bathroom and changing into a brand-new shirt Bryan kept in his desk for court appearances.

Bryan got a few hours' sleep himself, and then brought the file with him so he could watch over Sarah. He didn't think those thugs would be so bold as to enter the police station, but he'd been foolish enough to think she was safe going to the bathroom in a truck stop. He wasn't taking any chances.

He tossed the folder to one side. He had one thin thread that connected Mason to what was happening to Sarah. Why couldn't he let it go? Sarah looked peaceful as she slept. Without thinking, he reached over and touched her soft brown hair. Sarah stirred but didn't awaken.

Sandoval should be on shift soon. Though the chief had seemed more open to providing protection when he'd talked to him on the phone, Bryan had started to have mixed feelings about it. After last night, he didn't feel totally comfortable turning her over to some rookie officer. He wanted to be the one to protect her.

He grabbed the investigation folder. He flipped through the pages of the file, reliving each step forward in the investigation. Growing angry each time he thought of the legal roadblock Mason's lawyer had put in the way. Mason was a business owner known for making large donations to various community causes. He had the air of respectability and way too much money to spend on an unscrupulous legal team.

The real blow to the case was the disappearance of their key witness, a young Mexican woman named Eva who had been promised citizenship and a job. Instead, she had been moved from one factory job to another, locked in a room with dozens of other people every night. She escaped once she was moved to Montana and had come forward to the authorities. Bryan was pretty sure that Eva was dead, though they hadn't found the body.

The thick file slid off his lap and fell on the floor. He kneeled and gathered the papers back into a pile. Sarah stirred on the couch. She rolled so her face was away from him.

One of the papers caught his eyes. In preparation for the trial, they had subpoenaed all of Mason's financial records. The page he held was a list of Mason's assets. Mason owned houses in other states. He traveled out of the country often. And he was a mostly silent partner in several different businesses. His eyes scanned the list, resting on the words *part owner, Crazy Ray's used car dealership.*

Still clutching the paper, Bryan sat down on the carpet. So there was a connection between Mason and the man who approached Sarah at the fairgrounds. Excited, he paged through a phone book until he found the number for the car dealership. When he dialed, a message machine informed him that Ray had closed the shop and left for vacation as of today. Bryan clenched his teeth. How convenient and suspicious.

Through two sets of glass doors, Chief Sandoval made his way into the station.

Sandoval stopped as he passed the break room, his gaze resting momentarily on Sarah. "I heard you had quite a night."

Bryan stood up from the floor. "That's not half of it." He stepped outside the break room. Feeling a rising sense of anticipation, he placed the papers from the messed up file on his desk. "I think her missing brother connects back to the Mason case."

The chief drew his eyebrows together. "Keyes, you've got to let that Mason case go."

"No, listen to me. One of the men who tried to abduct her in the forest worked for Mason." Bryan stepped toward Sandoval. "And last night, the guy who approached her, probably to threaten her, when we were out looking for Crew is one of Mason's business partners, a man named Ray Mitchell—he owns a used car place."

"Those are tenuous connections. Have you contacted this Ray Mitchell?"

"His message machine says that he left for a vacation." Bryan stepped closer to the chief. "Reinstate me."

The chief pressed his lips together. "I'm not so sure you can see clearly where this case is concerned."

"Give me seventy-two hours. I'll make the case against him." And he'd make sure Sarah was safe. As important as it was to Bryan to see Mason brought to justice, it was also crucial to make sure Mason and his thugs would leave Sarah and her brother alone once and for all.

"And if you can't, you'll come back and be the good detective you've always been." The chief leaned toward him and looked him square in the eye. "Don't let your life be defined by this investigation."

Bryan nodded. "Just three days, that's all I need."

Sandoval rubbed his chin. "I'll put the paperwork through for your reinstatement."

Bryan slumped back down in his chair. He stared at the pile of papers, the sum total of the case against Mason. He'd have to call the Ranger Station and let them know he couldn't go back up in the tower. Once again, this case would be his focus.

Now that he was seeing connections, he wondered if this woman Crew was with might be Eva. Eva had dark hair, but she might be wearing a wig to disguise her appearance. Maybe he'd been too hasty in assuming she'd been killed. It would definitely explain why Crew's roommate said she was scared. But how would she have met Crew?

Sarah stirred and rolled back over. She opened her eyes.

Bryan leaned against the doorway that separated his office from the break room. "Hey, did you get rested up?"

"Guess I was pretty worn out." She sat up and ran her fingers through her curly hair. "So am I going to be able to go back to my house?"

She must have heard some of the conversation between him and Sandoval. "I don't know about that. I think it would be better if you stayed close to me."

"What about work? I'm supposed to go in today."

"Where do you work?"

"A place called Loving Hearts. It's a church-affiliated adoption service. Our office is downtown."

"Maybe you should ask for time off until we have assurance that we can keep you safe." Really the only guarantee she had for safety was if Mason was behind bars and his hired henchmen went with him.

"They need me at the office. I want to go in to work. I want my life back." She looked off to one side and let out a heavy breath.

"Sarah, you saw how serious these guys are."

She swiped a tear away from the corner of her eye. "I guess if that's how it has to be." She turned to face him. "So what do I do now?"

"You're safe in the station. I'll go with you if you need to go out."

"But you're going to be working on the case that has you so upset. This Tyler Mason guy." Her words carried traces of hurt.

"You heard what I said to Sandoval?"

"Is that the only reason you stayed with me? Because you thought there might be some connection between what Crew has gotten himself into and your big case?"

"Sarah, you have to know that that isn't true. After all we've been through in the last twenty hours you trust me more than that, don't you?"

Old insecurities plagued him. If she still saw their relationship in terms of what had happened ten years ago, the answer to that question would be no.

She stared at him, her eyes glazing. "I want to believe you."

Moved by her sadness, he leaned toward her, reaching out and covering her hand with his.

She pulled her hand away. "Your boss seems to think you don't see too clearly where this case is concerned, as if you're obsessed."

He felt the sting of her rejection. She couldn't receive the comfort he offered. "I just want Mason taken down. I don't like it when a bad guy gets away with acting like some sort of good citizen. If that makes me obsessed, then I guess I am."

"But that's your focus—arresting Mason. Not helping me, or finding Crew."

He could feel the wedge being driven between them. The unresolved pain that was always there would make it impossible for her to trust his motives. "I don't want to see you hurt."

She studied him for a long moment and then stared at the ceiling. "I'm hungry and I need to brush my teeth."

"I can have some takeout brought over. I've got a tube of toothpaste in my locker you can use. Problem solved."

Sarah smiled. "Like camping, right? You brush your teeth with your fingers."

He laughed. "I'll have one of the officers run across the street to the drugstore." He appreciated her sense of humor. This couldn't be easy for her. "Maybe we can get you back in your house before the day is over."

A take-out meal waited for Sarah when she returned from freshening up. Though a little big on her, the blue button-down shirt brought out the color in her eyes. The years had only enhanced her natural beauty.

He shuffled the papers he'd been poring over. "You look good."

Sarah blushed. "Thanks."

At least she could receive his compliment. Bryan worked through the afternoon while Sarah rested and read a book she borrowed from one of the other officers.

Her cell phone rang and she pulled it out. Her forehead wrinkled when she looked at the number. "Hello?"

The voice on the other end of the line sounded frantic.

Sarah leaned forward, her expression pensive. "Crew, is that you?"

Sarah could feel panic taking over, invading her mind and tensing her muscles as Crew spat out his words.

"I never meant for you to be hurt. I didn't know they would do something like this."

Anxiety built up inside her. Her brother was desperately afraid and not making much sense. "What's going on? Who are you in trouble with?"

"It's not me. I was only trying to do the right thing. I was only trying to help her."

Bryan stepped toward Sarah, leaning in so he could hear the conversation.

Sarah struggled to remain calm. "Who were you trying to help?"

"I wanted to do the right thing and it ended up getting you hurt. I'm so sorry."

"Crew, it's all right. Just tell me where you are. I can come and get you. The police will help protect you."

"I have to keep moving. There are spies everywhere."

Spies? What did Crew mean by that? "Tell me where you are now. Are you in town?" Sarah took in a breath. "I can be there in five minutes."

Sarah could hear Crew's breathing on the other end of the line.

"Crew, please. Where are you?"

"I can't stay here long." His voice trembled.

"Please tell me. I want to help."

"Lewis and Clark Park."

The line went dead.

Sarah pulled her phone away from her ear and turned to face Bryan. "He says he's at Lewis and Clark Park."

"I'll bring him in." Bryan headed toward the interior of the station. "I'll see if I can get some backup."

She grabbed his arm as he swept past. "I'm going with you."

"Sarah, I can't risk it."

She squeezed his arm. "He's my brother."

"I don't want you out in the open like that."

"I'm the one he trusts. If he sees a bunch of cops coming toward him, he might bolt."

Bryan studied Sarah for moment. "All right, you can come, but you stay close to me at all times."

Bryan led Sarah to the parking lot behind the station

where the patrol cars were. They jumped in and sped through downtown and several residential neighborhoods. Bryan grabbed the radio. "This is Unit Fourteen. I'm headed toward Lewis and Clark and requesting backup in bringing in a witness who may be in danger."

The dispatcher responded. "Unit Fourteen, Unit Nine is on the corner of Eighteenth and Grand. ETA is about five minutes."

"No sirens," Bryan commanded. "The man is approximately thirty years of age, dark curly hair, six feet tall." He clicked off his radio and glanced toward Sarah. "How does he dress?"

"I haven't seen him in months, but he has this pair of red high-tops that I gave him. I replace them whenever his current pair wears out. Oh, and he usually has a bandanna around his neck."

Bryan relayed the information to the other officers through the dispatcher.

A second patrol car responded saying they could be there in seven minutes.

Bryan pulled into the lot that surrounded Lewis and Clark Park. Sarah jumped out and surveyed the area. The park spread over five acres. A playground and a pavilion were close to the road. Beyond the rolling hills where college students sat under trees and played Frisbee was a second access road. The park had a river flowing through it, a natural amphitheater, and it connected to hiking trails.

Not all the park was visible from this vantage point. To the south the park connected with a cemetery and at the base of the rolling hills to the west was the public library, a popular hangout for some of Discovery's homeless. Would Crew be there? She should have gotten him to give her a more specific answer.

Another patrol car rolled by on the other road that bordered the park.

Bryan scanned the park. "This is a lot of acreage to cover. He didn't say where he'd be?"

"He said he had to keep moving." Sarah's fast walk turned into a jog as she searched for her brother. The more she searched without seeing him, the harder it was to breathe, as if her torso was wrapped in a tight cloth.

The beautiful, sunny afternoon brought an abundance of people out to the park. A group picnicked in the pavilion. Several bunches of children ran through the park or played on the slides and swings.

"He may have gone to the cemetery. Plenty of places to hide up there," Bryan suggested.

The other two police officers got out of their car. They waved in Bryan's direction and then proceeded to split off.

"He could be hiding behind a tree or down by the creek bed." She let out a breath. "I think he'll come out if he sees me."

"Why don't you try calling the number he phoned from?"

"He doesn't have a cell. It was probably a pay phone or the free phone in the library." Anxiety settled in her stomach like a rock. What if Crew had gotten scared and run away already?

"Hey, those guys look familiar." Bryan pointed across the park to three men headed down the hill toward the library.

"Yeah, from the shelter." Sarah took off at a dead run. "Hey, Eddie."

Eddie turned at the sound of his name. His eyes grew wide with recognition. The other two men continued on down the hill, giving nervous glances over their shoulders. Sarah's feet pounded across the lush grass of the park.

Sarah and Bryan were within twenty feet of Eddie when the sound of screeching tires on the road by the cemetery entrance drew their attention.

Two men, one of them Acne Scars, held a third man by his shoulders despite his attempts to struggle away. A van screeched to a halt. The sliding doors opened and the struggling man was tossed in. His abductors piled in behind him.

"That was Crew." Sarah took off running.

Bryan kept up with her as they sprinted up the hill. The van rolled toward the cemetery, not going fast enough to draw attention to itself.

They were out of breath by the time they made it to the top of the hill. The other two officers were not in sight and the third patrol car still had not arrived.

"They can't get out by way of the cemetery. They will have to circle around and come out another way. We might be able to cut them off at the park entrance."

They ran to the patrol car and jumped in. Bryan pulled away from the street.

Sarah scanned the landscape. Trees partially blocked her view of the entrance. "There it is."

The van rolled into view. It pulled out onto the street just as Bryan gained speed and slipped in behind it.

He grabbed the radio. "Our target has been taken in a dark van heading east on Babcock."

The van continued to move at a normal speed.

Sarah leaned close to the windshield. "Maybe we can sneak up on him."

"I wouldn't count on it. We're in a patrol car," said Bryan.

Traffic grew thicker the closer they got to the shopping district with four-lane through streets, fewer lights and big box stores.

The light up ahead turned yellow. The van sped up and raced through it.

Bryan hit the sirens. "He's on to us."

Cars pulled to the side of the street to get out of their

way. Bryan pressed the accelerator and zigzagged around the vehicles that were slow in reacting. The van sped through a red light. Two cars crashed into each other. Bryan swerved to avoid them.

He looked up ahead. "Where did it go?"

Sarah leaned forward, peering through the windshield. *Please, God, don't say we've lost them.*

Desperation settled in. She glanced up and down the street and at the side streets as they sped past. Sirens still flashing, Bryan slowed down.

She spotted the van rolling through the parking lot that connected with a home improvement store.

"There." She pointed.

The light turned green. Bryan zoomed toward the side street that connected with the parking lot. He radioed the other patrol cars advising them of his position. "You might want to get over here and see if we can block off the entrances."

Bryan rolled past the row of parked cars. None of them looked even remotely like the van. He turned and drove up the next row.

"Maybe we lost them," she whispered as a sense of despair overtook her. What would those men do to her brother? "We have to find him."

Bryan turned down another row. He pressed the brakes. Four car lengths from them stood the dark van.

Bryan picked up the radio and explained where he was. "Be advised. I have located the vehicle. I will wait for your arrival as suspects are likely armed and dangerous." He clicked off the radio and turned to Sarah. "You stay in this car."

Bryan slipped out of the driver's seat, crouching behind his open door. He drew his gun.

The other patrol car came to a stop on the opposite side of the van. Two officers got out, weapons drawn. Bryan lifted his chin, pointed toward the van and then held up two fingers. One officer remained behind his car door while the other moved forward to assist Bryan, who ran toward the van from the opposite direction.

With his gun drawn, he approached the driver's-side window. His arms slackened. He moved to the back of the vehicle when the officer appeared, shaking his head.

Fear twisted through Sarah. The men weren't in the front seat. What if they had gotten away? Bryan held up his gun. The other officer knocked on the van doors. He backed up without taking his eyes off the doors.

They waited a moment, both of them ready to shoot. Seconds ticked by. Sarah tensed. She brushed away images of Crew being harmed.

At Bryan's signal, the second officer strode forward and opened the van doors.

The interior was empty.

TEN

Sarah's footsteps pounded behind Bryan. Her voice was drenched with anguish. "Where is he? What happened?"

"They must have pulled into the lot here to switch vehicles." Bryan holstered his gun. Whether they'd planned it ahead of time or got the car into place when they realized they were being pursued, it was a clear indication that a mastermind was behind the whole operation.

"What do we do now? They're going to hurt him...or worse."

"We'll impound this vehicle for evidence," said the other officer. "I can take care of that."

"That won't help my brother." Sarah rested her palms on Bryan's chest, her eyes pleading. "We need to find those people now."

"We don't even know what kind of car they got away in." He could feel Sarah's desperation in every word she spoke. It was his desperation, too. This wasn't just about Mason. The clock was ticking for Crew. "We go to the source." Bryan stalked back toward the police car.

Sarah followed behind him. "What are you talking about?"

Once they were inside the car, Bryan gripped the steering wheel until his knuckles turned white. "I know Tyler

Mason is behind this. I'm going to go to him and get some answers now."

Sarah buckled her seat belt as Bryan sped through the parking lot.

"I'll take you back to the station," Bryan said.

"We don't have time for that."

Bryan tapped the steering wheel. Sending his business partner on a vacation was a good indication that Mason knew the spotlight was back on him. He doubted his appearance would come as a surprise to Mason. Sarah's appearance, on the other hand…who knew how the man would react to the arrival of the woman his thugs had been trying to capture for the past day? "No, it's not safe for you to come with me."

"I can't sit in that police station thinking about what my brother might be going through. I have to do something."

They were wasting precious time arguing. "All right, come with me, but stay in the reception area, where there are other people around. Mason wouldn't try anything, even on his home turf, if there's a chance he might be seen. He'll do everything to keep his hands clean."

"I want to meet this man who you think is behind all this."

"Sarah, I don't think you want to look into his eyes." They were the eyes of pure evil.

The force of his voice took any argument out of her. "All right, I'll do what you say."

He took several side streets into a business district. With each passing block, the rage inside him simmered to a boil.

"Do you think they were looking for Crew because of the woman his roommate saw him with, the woman he's trying to help?"

Bryan nodded as he watched the street addresses. "I suspect that they want information from him…probably about this woman." The idea that the woman might be

Eva, his missing witness, still tickled his brain. Why else would Mason work so hard to get at her?

He arrived at a building with doors marked for a book-keeping business and a massage studio. He parked in front of the office that said Workforhire.

Sarah rested her hand on his. "Are you sure you want to do this?"

Her touch soothed his ragged nerves. "We're out of options. We have to find your brother before it's too late. We need to stir things up. See if Mason blinks."

"Let's do this," Sarah said.

They swung open the door and stepped into a reception area done in rich browns and tans. A man and a woman both dressed in suits sat on the high-end leather couches. Bryan's investigation revealed that Mason had a number of legitimate clients. But the math didn't work out for the kind of assets Mason owned compared to the number of people who openly found work through his agency. Most of the other businesses Mason owned barely broke even.

Sarah took a seat on the couch. Bryan stalked over to the receptionist, a twenty-something blonde with short, spiky hair. She adjusted her headset as Bryan approached. Her eyes grew wide with recognition. He'd come to this office several times when he'd been running the investigation.

No doubt, Mason had trained her in the latest diversion and stall tactics if he were to show up. He skirted past her without even making eye contact.

"Sir, where are you going?"

Bryan strode toward an ornate wooden door. He pushed it open.

Mason looked up from his keyboard. His mouth formed a perfect O shape. His cold gray eyes gave away nothing.

The receptionist scurried up behind Bryan, directing her comments to Mason. "I tried to stop him."

"It's all right, Cassandra. It seems Officer Keyes is quite

adamant about talking to me. Close the door on your way out." His voice was icy, his words clipped.

Cassandra backed out, easing the door shut.

Mason laced his fingers together. His skin was tanning-booth orange and his dark eyebrows stood in sharp contrast to his brassy blond hair. "I guess I can't call you Officer Keyes. The last I heard, you were babysitting a forest."

Mason's condescending tone was calculated to get a rise out of him. The man wanted him to lose control. Despite the rage that smoldered inside, Bryan wasn't about to take the bait. "Well, I'm back on the force."

Mason made a clicking noise with his tongue. "Oh, good, back to writing tickets for the jaywalkers."

Bryan planted his feet. "I know that you're responsible for Crew Langston being kidnapped."

Mason raised his eyebrows. "I've never heard of the man." The nervous tapping of his fingers on the desk gave him away. He was lying.

Bryan lunged toward Mason's desk. "What have you done with him?"

Mason stood up. "Officer Keyes, why must you persist in this line of questioning?" Despite the plastic smile, his voice had a waver to it. Mason was behind all of this. He was sure of it now.

Bryan gritted his teeth. "If anything happens to him, I'll see to it that it's hung around your neck."

Mason skirted around his desk and sat on the corner. "And I told you I've never heard of the man." He lifted his chin in a show of superiority.

Bryan's rage threatened to explode.

Keep your cool. The last thing you want is for him to file assault charges.

Bryan leaned toward him. "What has he done? Did a high school dropout junkie actually manage to get one over on you?"

Mason blinked and looked away. Bryan detected a flicker of emotion. Mason was good at hiding his true motives. But the mask had fallen away for a second, revealing fear. Somehow, Crew had managed to outsmart the mighty Tyler Mason.

"This is a business, Mr. Keyes. I don't appreciate your threatening attitude. Unless you have need of some temporary labor or would like to sign up for our service, I suggest you leave."

The nerve. Mason's holier-than-thou posturing made his blood boil. He had to get out before he took a swing at Mason. "If a hair on Crew Langston's head is harmed, I will come after you and nail you to the wall."

"You tried that once, Officer Keyes." His words dripped with sarcasm. "It's hard to send an innocent man to jail. And that's what I am—an innocent man. So I suggest you quit harassing me."

Bryan's hand curled into a fist. His voice turned low and husky. "I'll see myself out."

Sarah rose to her feet when he came to the reception area. She waited until they were outside before she spoke.

"Did he say anything about Crew?"

"It's what he didn't say. I'm more convinced than ever that he's behind this," Bryan said.

"Where do we go now? How does this help us find Crew?"

Bryan mulled through the possibilities. "I stirred up Mason. Let's watch this place and see if he leaves...sends someone out to check on things. My guess is he'll use the receptionist."

"They'd want to take him somewhere they could question him and not be disturbed." Sarah opened the passenger-side door. She rested her elbow on the hood of the car, a note of urgency laced through her words. "We don't have much time. I doubt their methods of questioning are humane."

"I know, but what are we going to do? Search every building in town?" Frustration formed a tight knot at the base of his neck. "Our best bet is to see how Mason reacts. He has to lead us to them."

Sarah pressed her lips together and hung her head. He understood the sense of helplessness she must be wrestling with.

She looked off into the distance. "I guess they won't kill him as long as he doesn't tell them what he knows. He'll hold out. My brother is more stubborn than me." She slipped into the car.

After he sat behind the wheel, Bryan turned the key in the ignition and pulled the patrol car into an out-of-the-way spot. "I'm going to call the station, have them bring over something less conspicuous."

Within ten minutes, an officer had shown up with an unmarked car, a white sedan. Bryan and Sarah waited through the early evening. The sun was low in the sky when Cassandra emerged through the front doors. They tailed Cassandra around town while she stopped at several businesses and an office supply place. None of the buildings she entered were likely candidates for holding Crew.

Bryan wondered if he'd made a bad call when the police radio sparked to life.

"Unit Nine, I've got a report of a disturbance. Car dealership on Nineteenth and Main. Neighbor saw lights flash on and off. Place is supposed to be closed."

Bryan grabbed the radio. "This is Unit Fourteen. I'm taking that call. We're en route."

"Affirmative," dispatch responded. "Are you in the neighborhood?"

"Close enough. Send backup. No sirens." Bryan sped

up the car. "This is more than a disturbance." He hung up the radio.

Sarah looked at him, her eyes questioning.

"The dealership on the corner of Main and Nineteenth is Crazy Ray's. That's got to be where they took him."

ELEVEN

Sarah gripped the armrest as Bryan sped down Nineteenth Street. The businesses on this end of town were all on one- and two-acre lots, mostly RV and motorcycle dealerships and home repair stores. They passed two lots that had buildings with For Sale signs. He pressed the brakes as they rolled into Crazy Ray's, past rows and rows of cars. Bryan killed the headlights and slowed to a snail's pace. He stopped. "Let's not park too close. You stay here. My backup should be here any second."

"Okay." She wasn't about to wait this out in the car. Crew was her brother. But they didn't have time for arguments. She'd do exactly what he'd said—she would stay there…right up until she got up and left. He hadn't specified how *long* she should stay there, after all.

She waited until Bryan was twenty feet from the building before pushing open her own door. She sprinted with a light step, came up behind Bryan and placed her hand on his back.

"I should have guessed you weren't going to stay in the car," he whispered.

She stared out into the lot. Where was that backup?

Bryan drew his gun. The dealership was dark. A note on the door indicated the store was closed while the owner was on vacation.

Another car with lights turned off rolled through the lot. That must be their backup. Two officers, barely shadows in the twilight, exited the car. Responding to Bryan's hand signals, they disappeared around the side of the building.

Bryan pushed on the front door. It opened. A place like this probably had all kinds of security and an alarm system—which had been turned off. A clear sign that somebody was here.

Bryan slipped inside, Sarah pressed close behind him. Darkness covered the showroom floor. Cars appeared in silhouette.

Bryan raced over to a room marked Office. "Stand back and to the side." His whisper was forceful.

Sarah pressed against the wall.

He tried the doorknob. "Locked."

Sarah turned her head. To her side was a white door, slightly ajar. She tugged on Bryan's sleeve and pointed.

He tiptoed across the floor. Resting his back against the wall, he pushed the door open, revealing a repair shop connected to the dealership. She could discern only the outlines of cars and equipment. No movement, no light. Only silence.

Yet, the pathway of unlocked doors suggested this was the way the perpetrators had come. Could they have left already?

Her heart drummed wildly, sweat snaked down her back.

A muffled thud emanated from a corner of the room.

A single word boomed through the space. "Police."

More noise, banging, louder this time.

Bryan hit the lights. The main area contained only an elevated car.

"There!" said Sarah, pointing at the door across the room. Bryan took the lead, kicking the door in. An officer lay on the floor by the door that led outside, not moving.

She gasped. There was blood everywhere. Not just on the floor by the downed police officer. She saw blood on a tan leather chair. Duct tape around the arms of the chair.

The second officer burst through the outside door.

Tires screeched in the parking lot.

"I got this," the officer said, leaning over his partner. "You go catch those guys."

Bryan pulled her through the door and dragged her to the car. She'd gone numb.

That was Crew's blood in there.

Though she had no clear memory of her actions, she must have gotten in the car. She shook herself free of emotional paralysis at the moment Bryan pulled out of the lot onto the street. Red taillights burned in front of them.

Bryan stayed close to the brown car as it sped through the streets up until a delivery truck pulled out from a side road, slipping in between them right before they came to a stop at a red light.

Bryan angled his head. "I can't see him."

Though the delivery truck blocked their view, the light must have turned green. The row of cars eased forward.

Bryan rolled down the window and leaned out. "He switched lanes. He's turning." Bryan cranked the wheel, pulling out of the line of stopped traffic. Several cars honked as he headed up the street where a green arrow indicated cars could make a left turn.

Sarah scanned the street. Though traffic was light at this hour, it was hard to find the other car. Then she caught sight of a brown vehicle turning off onto a side street, traveling faster than the flow of traffic. Bryan closed the distance between them. He radioed his position and the direction the car was going. Sirens sounded in the distance. The car doubled back toward Crazy Ray's but abruptly turned into one of the for-sale lots, a former car repair place. Taillights disappeared around the empty building.

Bryan followed as the sirens grew louder. They sped around the corner. Her vision filled with taillights. The thugs had stopped for some reason, but now they were trying to get up to speed again.

Sarah searched the dark lot. "Stop, I think they dumped him."

Bryan didn't slow down. An engine roared as the assailants' car rolled back out onto the road. "Why would they push him out?"

She searched the dark lot. "Maybe because they knew they were going to be caught. I saw them come to a full stop." She discerned a lump toward the edge of the lot. Her heart squeezed tight.

Bryan stopped the car and radioed the patrol unit to continue up the road after the car. "We were the ones with the best chance of catching them. Those guys will get into the flow of traffic and be lost. I hope you're right about them dumping Crew."

Sarah pushed the door open.

In the dim light, it was hard to see anything. Frantic, Sarah sprinted toward the motionless shadow at the edge of the lot.

They had taken a gamble by not following the car. She could only hope—and pray—that it would pay off.

Please, God, let it be Crew.

As she drew closer, she was able to see the outline of a man lying on the ground, still not moving. Her heart stopped. Time seemed to slow down as she took the remaining steps toward the body.

"Crew? It's me." No response. She dropped to her knees.

With trembling fingers, she touched his neck. A faint pulse pushed back. The coppery scent of blood filled her nostrils. "Hang in there. We'll get you help."

Behind her, she could hear Bryan already calling for an ambulance.

Bryan approached and kneeled beside her. Leaning closer to Crew, he placed his palm on Crew's chest, examined the blood on his clothes and then took his hand and squeezed it. "He's pretty beat up." His voice was filled with indignation.

Sarah released a cry. "I know."

In the distance, the sirens cut through the stillness of the night.

Moments later, the flashing light turned into the lot. Bryan ran out to meet the ambulance and direct them to where Sarah waited with Crew.

Two EMTs, a man and a woman, carried a stretcher over to them. When the man shone a flashlight on Crew's face, the amount of crusted dried blood shocked her.

Crew was lifted onto the stretcher.

"I'll ride in the ambulance." Her voice came out monotone. Shock had settled in. She felt only numbness.

Bryan rested a hand on her shoulder. "I'll be right behind you."

She draped her hand over his. "Thank you."

They trotted across the broken concrete to where the ambulance waited. She squinted at the bright lights as she climbed in and sat beside Crew. He'd been hooked up to an IV, but remained motionless, with his eyes closed.

She touched his thick, dark hair.

Please, God, don't let him die.

She studied Crew. His shirt was bloody, his face bruised. A thousand memories scrolled through her head. She'd been five and Crew had been seven when their parents died. Their grandmother had taken them in until she died. After that, it had been a series of foster homes. Some good, some not so good. Crew had been the one constant in her life.

They pulled up to the emergency room doors. Sarah stepped out and watched as they unloaded the stretcher.

She glanced around the lot and at the entrances. No sign of Bryan.

Sarah entered through the doors where they'd taken her brother.

The woman at the check-in desk stood up. "Ma'am, it would be best if you waited until the doctor came out to talk to you."

"But I want to be with my brother."

"They have to determine the extent of his injuries and what needs to be done." The woman handed her a clipboard. "In the meantime, why don't you fill out this information about your brother."

With a heavy heart, Sarah sat down in the waiting room. She stared at the form on the clipboard. Health Insurance, Address, Place of Employment—all normal things that most people took for granted. She tossed the form aside. She didn't want to think about this right now.

She paced. She found a vending machine with snacks and a soda. She paced some more.

She slumped down in the chair and stared out at the dark night. Bryan should be here by now.

What had delayed him?

The taillight of the ambulance had no sooner slipped out of view over a hill when Bryan's phone buzzed with a new text. He pulled over, expecting it to be from Sarah.

I suggest you stop your investigation right now.

No need to sign that one. Mason was up to his old tricks. Of course, it would be from a number that couldn't be traced back to him. The guy was good at covering his tracks.

The text didn't scare him. It fueled his anger and indignation. He'd been running away from Mason's thugs when he'd climbed up into that fire tower with Sarah, and it seemed like he'd been running in one way or another ever since. No more.

If it was the last thing he ever did and the hardest thing he did, he would see to it that Mason went to jail so that no one would have to fear him or his cohorts ever again.

And he was starting to think he was getting pretty close. Mason was becoming either sloppy or desperate. Setting Crazy Ray's up as a torture chamber wasn't too smart. Mason had to know they'd linked the dealership to him or he wouldn't have sent Ray on *vacation* where he couldn't talk.

He turned his steering wheel and entered the flow of traffic. Mason's thugs hadn't killed Crew, but they had dumped him and left him for dead. Had Crew finally given them the information they wanted? Or had they given up? They knew they were being tailed. Maybe they'd decided Crew's information wasn't worth getting caught over.

The road curved as he headed uphill. The hospital was built next to the hiking trails that connected with Lewis and Clark Park. He pulled into the hospital parking lot. Though the lot wasn't as full as it would have been during the day, he had to park a ways from the emergency room doors.

As he approached the emergency room, a man in scrubs came through the hospital's sliding doors. "Are you Bryan Keyes?"

"Yeah." How did this guy know his name?

"Sarah Langston asked me to keep an eye out for you. She misplaced her phone. They've taken her brother to surgery on the third floor. There's a waiting room up there right through the main entrance. She wanted you to know that you'll find her there."

Nodding his understanding, Bryan passed through the sliding doors. A woman with her head bent over a book sat at the registration desk. He walked over to the elevator, stepped in and pushed the button for the third floor.

Moments later, the doors slid open. The second he stepped out on the carpet, Bryan knew something was wrong.

At this time of night, he didn't expect a huge staff, but no one occupied the nurses' station. Bryan strode toward the hallway. Empty. A huge piece of plastic had been stapled across an opening at the end of the hallway along with a sign that read Closed For Construction.

He'd been set up.

Bryan turned and bolted for the elevator.

Why the misdirection? Had they come back to finish Crew off and didn't want him interfering? Or…oh, no, were they after Sarah again and wanted him out of the way?

Glancing side to side, he waited for the elevator doors to open.

Footsteps pounded behind him. He whirled around, ready to land a blow. The assailant, his old buddy Deep Voice, grabbed his arm. A second man came up from behind.

He had only a moment to register the needle sinking into his biceps before he collapsed to the floor.

TWELVE

"Miss Langston?"

Someone shook her shoulder. She opened her eyes. Predawn light streamed through the window. She'd been asleep on the waiting room couch for hours.

She looked up at the woman who had awakened her. Dressed as a nurse, she was middle-aged with kind eyes.

"Your brother is stabilized. He's got some fractured ribs and lacerations. The thing we are most concerned about is his brain. He received severe blows to the head. We'll have to watch him for several days to determine the extent of the damage."

"Is he conscious?"

The nurse shook her head. "You're welcome to go in and sit with him. Room 117."

Sarah stood up. Her head still hadn't cleared from the fog of sleep. Bryan wasn't in the waiting room. As she made her way down the hall, she tried his cell phone. No answer. Sarah pushed open the door of 117.

Crew looked peaceful. The blood had been cleaned off him and replaced with clean white bandages around his head and on his hand. A nurse checked an IV and pulled the blankets up higher on his chest. Beside the bed on a tray sat a wallet, a watch and a creased picture of her and Crew. They must have tossed out the bloody bandanna.

The nurse pulled a chair from a corner of the room. "Sometimes it helps if you talk to them. The jury is still out on how much someone in a coma can hear."

Sarah winced at the word *coma*.

"I'm sure the talking won't be in vain. I've seen amazing recoveries in my time." The nurse patted Crew's head and left, her soft-soled shoes barely making any noise as she crossed the room.

Sarah leaned over the bed and took Crew's hand in her own. "Hey, big brother." His fingers were as cold to the touch as porcelain. She spoke some more to him about shared childhood memories. Overcome with sorrow, she stepped away from the hospital bed. She had to do something or the sadness and fear for Crew's future would consume her.

Finding Bryan seemed like the easiest task. But when she tried calling again, he still wasn't picking up. Maybe he'd been called to another job?

Sarah cleared her throat and dialed the police station. "Hello, I'm trying to locate Officer Bryan Keyes. Has he come by there or called in?"

"Not that I noticed, and he's not on the roster yet," said the desk sergeant.

"Can you have him call me if he does come in?" Sarah gave her name and number and hung up.

A chill that had nothing to do with the room permeated her skin. What had happened to Bryan?

She studied her phone. With two phone calls she had exhausted the possibilities of who she could contact. She didn't know anything about Bryan anymore—who his friends were, who was important in his life. Ten years ago, he had been her whole world.

Her gaze traveled over to the tray that contained all of Crew's worldly possessions. A revelation crept into her head. No phone.

Crew had called her when she was at the station, but he had no cell phone in his possession. He could have used a pay phone or the free one at the library, but...what if he'd simply borrowed a phone from someone? It was worth checking. She clicked through her phone until the number she was looking for came up. She dialed it.

"Hello?"

She recognized the voice. "Eddie, is that you?"

The line went dead.

She wandered the room. No use calling back; he'd check the number. Eddie had been leaving the park when Crew was taken, and he was the one who had lured her into the fairgrounds building. Why didn't he want to talk to her? She remembered what Crew had said about there being spies everywhere. At the time it had seemed paranoid, but now...

She stared out the window. The tall street lamp glowed in the early morning light. She stepped a little closer to the window. Down below, Bryan's white sedan stood out. Panic flooded through her. Bryan had made it to the hospital. So where was he?

Sarah stroked Crew's cheek and kissed his forehead. "Hang in there."

She ran out into the hallway and back to the emergency room check-in desk. The admin woman was the same one who had been on duty when Crew was brought in.

"Did a man come through here looking for me, Sarah Langston? He's tall, broad shoulders, dark brown hair. He had on a black T-shirt."

The woman shook her head. "Sorry. We had an abundance of senior citizens and teenagers last night but no one who looked like that."

Sarah ran out to the white sedan. Locked. Empty.

Her hands were shaking when she dialed directly into the police station.

"Discovery Police Station." The same desk sergeant she had talked to earlier.

Sarah struggled to speak in a calm voice. "I think Bryan Keyes is missing. He was supposed to meet me at the hospital, but something must have happened to him. His car is here, but he never came into the E.R. That was hours ago."

"I'll send a unit over."

Sarah hung up and searched the lot. Where else would he have gone? The pharmacy and doctors' offices were all closed at night. Her gaze rested on the general registration and admittance area, separate from the E.R.

She hurried over to the sliding glass doors and stepped onto the carpet.

A lone woman sat behind her computer. "Can I help you?"

"Were you working about five or six hours ago?"

"Yes, I was. I get off shift in about forty-five minutes."

"Did a man about my age come through here?"

She thought for a moment. "Tall guy, dark shirt? Sort of messy handsome look?"

Sarah nodded.

"We don't get that much traffic. I thought it was odd that he didn't ask me for directions. He went straight for the elevator like he knew where he was going."

"Where could he have gone?"

"The third floor on this wing is under construction, so he probably went up to the second floor."

"There's no one on the third floor?" Realization spread through her.

The admin lady furled her forehead. "Not at night. The construction guys show up around nine."

Sarah darted over to the elevator. Bryan hadn't gone to the second floor. He'd been lured to the third floor; she was sure of it. As the elevator rose, she realized she probably should have waited for the police to show up. But she couldn't just sit around, not knowing if Bryan was up there. If he was hurt. If he needed her help.

She pulled her key ring from her purse and adjusted the pepper spray in her hand. The door slid open. Sarah stepped onto the carpet. Treading lightly, she walked over to the nurses' station.

A door whooshed open down the hall. The crinkle of thick plastic pressed on her ears. Sarah ducked behind the high counter of the nurses' station and peeked around to watch as a man stalked past, his footfall heavy on the floor.

She lifted her head a few inches above the counter. She saw the man from the back as he stared at the elevator— muscular, thick neck…it was Deep Voice, the guy who had taken her into the forest to kill her.

Bryan had to be around here somewhere. She scampered on all fours toward the wall of plastic. Carefully lifting the plastic at the corner, she cringed at each noise as she scooted through.

Sarah came out into an expansive open area where the walls had been gutted, the floors torn up and building materials occupied most of the floor space. She ran around a stack of drywall. Bryan slumped in a corner of the room. His chin resting on his chest, his shirt torn, hands tied in front of him.

"Bryan."

He lifted his head, but it wobbled on his neck. His eyes were unfocused. His breathing labored.

"Let's get you out of here."

She had only minutes before the guard came back.

"Knife in my pocket." Bryan bent his head, indicating the pocket of his jeans.

She dug out the pocketknife and cut him free. She angled underneath his shoulder and helped him stand. They couldn't go back to the elevator. With Bryan limping along, she searched the room. There had to be a stairwell around here somewhere.

She spotted it just as she heard the crinkling of plastic. No way could they outrun the guard. Sarah flung open the door of the stairwell. She let go of Bryan, allowing him to slump to the floor.

Then she waited, holding the pepper spray in her trembling hand.

Pounding footsteps. The stairwell door swung open. She aimed and pressed the button. Deep Voice shrieked, groaned in pain. Stepping over him, she pressed the door shut and helped Bryan get to his feet.

He was coming around, more able to walk though still dizzy. They had just made it to the second floor landing when the door above them swung open. Deep Voice shouted down at them, his voice bouncing off the tight walls. The time between footsteps indicated he couldn't see clearly.

Sarah pushed open the door and stepped out onto a floor that appeared abandoned, as well. The signs on the doors indicated that these were specialists' offices. The elevator was at the end of the hall. She pushed the button for the first floor. Bryan leaned against the wall for support.

Behind them, the stairwell door burst open. Deep Voice stumbled toward them, swaying a bit and stopping to rub his eyes.

The elevator doors remained shut.

The thug loomed closer to them.

Sarah pushed the button again.

He was within twenty feet. His reddened face stood in sharp contrast to his snarling mouth that revealed yellow teeth.

The doors swung open. Bryan stumbled inside, but when she moved to follow, Deep Voice grabbed her shirttail and held her back. Bryan leapt toward her, gathering her in his arms. He pulled her free and pushed the man. Caught off guard, the thug stumbled backward and the elevator doors slid closed.

The elevator descended and Bryan held her while he leaned against the wall, strong arms surrounding her. She rested her palm on his chest where she could feel his heart racing. She tilted her head and looked into his eyes. "What happened to you?" Her voice came out in a breathless whisper.

Still not totally free from whatever they had drugged him with, Bryan blinked several times. "They *encouraged* me to drop the investigation. And I think they wanted me out of commission. When I got to the hospital, someone was waiting outside, dressed in scrubs, to tell me you were waiting for me on the third floor. Once I showed up, they drugged me."

"But they didn't try to kill you."

"I'm sure they would have eventually, but not before I could be used to somehow get them access to you or Crew." The elevator doors opened. Bryan pushed away from the wall. "Is Crew still…?"

She pulled free of his embrace. "Yes, he's alive—but not conscious."

Strength returned to Bryan's voice. "We better get over there. I don't think he's safe."

THIRTEEN

Bryan's head still felt fuzzy from the drugs that had left him incapacitated but conscious. He tried as best he could to scan for any signs of danger.

Sarah squeezed his hand and pulled him down a hallway. "His room is up here." Her voice filled with urgency.

From inside the room, a woman screamed. A man in scrubs emerged. The same man who had misdirected Bryan before. His eyes grew wide at the sight of Bryan. He turned and bolted. Bryan ran after him, but in his weakened state he knew he wouldn't be able to keep up. The man disappeared around a corner.

Bryan braced his hand against a wall, gasping for breath. He returned to the room where a nurse and Sarah both leaned over Crew.

"Is he…?"

"When I came in here…" The nurse put a trembling hand to her mouth. "That man was holding Mr. Langston by the collar and slapping him."

Bryan approached the hospital bed. Crew lay with his eyes closed, still unconscious. "Do you know who he is?"

"He's not anyone I've ever seen on shift," said the nurse.

Bryan pulled Sarah aside while the nurse continued to fuss over Crew. "I don't think Crew told those guys what they wanted to know. That's why they came back here. You heard what the nurse said. That guy could have used the opportunity to kill Crew, but he didn't. Instead, he tried to wake him up."

"So they didn't toss him out of the car because they were finished with him."

"They must have panicked because we were closing in on them," Bryan said. "I'm sure Mason encouraged them to finish their mission."

The nurse left the room.

"Staff watched him pretty close through the night. This was probably the first chance they had to find him alone." Sarah clutched Bryan's shirt and gazed up into his eyes. "What are we going to do?"

"I'll make sure there's an armed guard outside Crew's door."

Sarah glanced out a window. "I called into the station when I couldn't find you. They should be here by now."

"We'll go find them and post one outside Crew's door until we line up something more permanent," Bryan said. "I'm not sure what our next move should be."

"I think we need to find Eddie. He loaned Crew his phone to call me. He's the one who lured me into that building. I think he knows something."

Bryan rushed out to the nurses' station and told them to send the policemen to Crew's room when they showed up.

They stayed in Crew's room while they waited for the officers to arrive.

Sarah stood up. "Are you hungry? I can grab you a snack out of the vending machine."

"Anything to fill the hole in my stomach." His throat was parched. "Mostly, I could use some water."

Sarah left and returned a moment later with a container of bottled water and several bags of chips. He gulped the water.

She scooted the second chair toward him, leaned in

and touched a bump on his head he'd gotten courtesy of Mason's thugs.

"What exactly did they do to you?" Her fingers were softer than rose petals.

"I didn't get the impression they wanted to beat any information out of me. They wanted to incapacitate me. I'm a little foggy on the details. One of them grabbed my chin and said something about me going back to the fire tower and leaving the police force, about how any investigation I was pursuing would only lead to trouble."

"But he didn't use Tyler Mason's name."

"Of course not. It was intended as a veiled threat." Bryan clenched his teeth. "Mason won't tie himself to any of this."

The officers arrived. Bryan gave them instructions as well as a description of the man who had impersonated medical personnel.

In the parking lot, morning sun lightened up the sky and warmed the air. Bryan rubbed his eyes.

Sarah offered him a sympathetic glance. "You must be tired."

"Believe it or not, I slept some up on that hospital floor." He climbed into the car and started it. "Where can we find this Eddie guy?"

"It's still early. Lots of homeless people sleep down by the river in the summer. Some of them hang out at the library later in the day."

"We'll try the river first." Bryan drove for several blocks. He checked his rearview mirror. "We have a friend."

Sarah craned her neck. "How long has he been on us?"

"Since we left the hospital. He disappears and then shows up a couple of blocks later. He thinks he's being sneaky." Bryan turned away from the direction of the river. "Let's lose him for good."

He took the first on-ramp that led out to the highway. Bryan pressed the gas and wove through traffic.

"I can still see him back there." Her words were saturated with tension.

He increased his speed, then slowed and took the exit leading back into town without signaling first. The dark car switched lanes and followed.

Bryan's frustration grew. "When are these guys going to give up?"

"Can you lose him?" Sarah asked.

"Sure, but I don't know what good it will do. Even when we manage to lose them for a little while, they always seem to have a good idea of where we're going next, so they can track us from there."

Sarah touched his forearm. "I have an idea where we could go that they wouldn't expect—Naomi's Place."

Bryan's back stiffened at the name of the pregnancy counseling center they'd gone to when Sarah had become pregnant. His throat clamped shut. He couldn't respond to her suggestion.

She squeezed his arm. "The director will help us. We can hide out there until we're in the clear."

He felt tightness in his chest. Going back there would only remind him of how he had failed Sarah ten years ago. "You're in touch with her, are you?"

"Yes, I work for an adoption agency, remember?"

Bryan clenched his teeth. There must be other places they could go to escape the endless cycle of being tailed.

"We've got to go someplace they're not expecting us to go. Naomi might be able to loan us a different car. We could slip out the back," Sarah said.

Bryan expelled a breath. Sarah had a point. They needed to do something unexpected. Something Mason couldn't anticipate. "Is he behind us now?"

She glanced out the back window. "Not that I can see. Now is our chance."

Bryan turned up a side street. "If he catches up with us, the plan is off." He wove through several more residential streets.

Naomi's Place was an old school that had been converted into a residence. Hedges and trees concealed much of the building from view. Bryan pulled around to the back.

Sarah took the lead, knocking on the door. A young girl, obviously pregnant, answered the door.

"We need to talk to Naomi. Tell her Sarah Langston is here."

The girl eyed Bryan suspiciously. "I'll go get her. You can wait in the living room."

They walked past an industrial-sized kitchen where several girls laughed and joked with an older woman while they did dishes.

The girl led them into a huge room filled with what looked like secondhand furniture. The long, narrow room with several seating areas had probably been a classroom at one time. Bryan sat down on a plush couch as a knot of anxiety formed in his stomach. This was a trip down memory lane he did not want to take.

Though Sarah had lived here until their baby had been born, he had come only twice for counseling. Memories flooded his mind. He recalled the pressure his parents had put on him. They had never liked Sarah. They wanted the whole thing washed away as though it had never happened. He'd been too young to stand up for himself and then he'd taken his frustration out on Sarah, giving her the silent treatment when she needed his support.

He shifted in his chair, crossing and uncrossing his legs. Then he bolted up to his feet.

Sarah gazed up at him. "This place might not have good

memories for you. But it does for me. I found kindness and God's love here."

"Let's get this over with."

She rose to her feet and met his gaze. "We never could have given her the life she deserved, Bryan. We were just kids."

He slumped down in the chair, ran his hands through his hair. He studied her for a moment. The soft angles of her face, her creamy skin and bright eyes. "I know that now. I didn't know it when I was seventeen. I guess I had this dumb idea that we could have been some sort of happy family, but Mom and Day were just so…"

"Your parents were right."

Her answer shocked him.

"They were not nice to me. But they were right. The adoption gave all three of us a chance at a good life."

He looked into Sarah's clear, bright eyes. She seemed to have made peace with the past, even if he couldn't.

A tall woman with dark hair streaked with gray stood in the entryway. "Sarah, how good to see you and…" She studied Bryan for a moment. "Oh, my, the name escapes me, but I remember you." She looked again at Sarah, a faint smile forming on her face.

Sarah put her hands up. "Naomi, it's not what you think. We're not…" Color rose up in her cheeks.

Bryan stood up. "We need your help with a police matter." Bryan flashed his badge. "It's a long story, but if we could borrow your car and leave ours here, we'd really appreciate it."

Naomi drew her eyebrows together and studied Bryan for a moment.

"Sarah's in some danger," Bryan said.

Naomi slowly nodded. "Sure, Sarah, if that's all you need. I'll go get my key from my office." She left the room and returned a moment later, holding the key and a photograph. "What's so strange about you coming by is that I was just thinking about you. I've been sending out invitations for a reunion. You girls who were here that winter ten years ago had such a wonderful bond, I thought it might be nice for you to get together again. You remember these girls."

She handed Sarah the photograph. Bryan peered over her shoulder. Sixteen-year-old Sarah with two other girls sitting in front of a Christmas tree.

"I didn't have any trouble finding Rochelle. She still lives here in town, but we have no way of contacting Clarissa. The three of you were so close. I don't suppose she stayed in touch with you?"

Sarah shook her head. "I got a postcard from her about a year after she left. She had a job in California. After that, nothing."

She looked at Sarah. "I do hope to see you here for the get-together." She handed the keys to Bryan. "It's the little blue car. Maybe we'll see you here, too."

He shrugged noncommittally to avoid being rude. After all, she was helping them, and she seemed to be very important to Sarah. But at the same time he knew he didn't want to come back here. The place was a reminder of the hole inside him over the life that might have been. The family he could have had if they hadn't rushed things.

Bryan took his house key off the key ring and then handed the rest over to Naomi. "In case you need to go anywhere. We'll make arrangements to get the car back to you."

They walked out to the gravel lot where the car was parked. Neither of them said anything for several blocks. He still felt stirred up, unable to shake the regret that plagued him.

"Should we try the river first?" asked Sarah. "Eddie

hung up when I called him. He might not be anxious to see us."

"Or maybe he's dying to tell us what he knows," Bryan said. "Get that burden off his chest."

"Let's hope that's what it is." Sarah looked at the pedestrians on the street. "Eddie isn't a bad person. I'm not sure what's going on with him."

Bryan parked some distance from the river. He got out of the car and waited for Sarah. At this hour, most of the homeless had wandered toward the center of town to sit in the park or the library. They walked past smoldering fires from the evening before. A man with a thick beard and tangled white hair slipped deeper into the trees when he saw them.

"Maybe we're too late, huh?"

"No, I think we're just in time." Bryan pointed to a man sleeping beneath a piece of cardboard. His distinctive dress shoes stuck out from under the edge of the cardboard.

Sarah stopped. Her eyes filled with fear. "He's not moving," she said in a harsh whisper.

Mason couldn't have gotten to him first. Or could he? Bryan stalked toward the prone figure. He lifted the cardboard, searching for signs of life. Eddie lay still with his eyes closed, hands at his side.

Sarah released a sharp half breath.

Bryan leaned closer to the prone man. He detected the slight up and down motion of Eddie's chest. He poked him in the shoulder. Eddie sat bolt upright, his eyes growing round at the sight of them.

He angled away from Bryan, intending to get to his feet.

Bryan grabbed his arm and pulled him down. "Oh, no, you don't."

Eddie yelped with exaggerated pain, massaging his arm where Bryan had touched him.

"Eddie, we need to talk to you about Crew. I already

know you loaned him your phone when you two were in the park yesterday." Sarah got down on her knees, so she could look Eddie in the eye.

Eddie spat out his words. "He wanted to talk to you. I didn't have anything to do with those men taking him. That wasn't me. No." Eddie grimaced, becoming more agitated. "Somebody else did that."

"Is that what Crew meant when he said there were spies?" Sarah's soft voice seemed to calm Eddie a little.

"For maybe five days now, there's been guys around the river and down at the shelter trying to find Crew, offering money to anyone who knew anything and was willing to talk." Eddie wrung his hands. "Not me, I wouldn't take it."

So anybody who saw Crew in the park could have tipped off Mason's men.

"But you dragged me to the fairgrounds when you knew full well Crew wasn't there." Sarah's voice held no judgment.

Eddie hung his head. "The guy gave me fifty bucks. He said he wasn't going to hurt you." Eddie fidgeted and wiggled. "Can I go now?"

Sarah draped her hand over Eddie's. "We know you wanted to help Crew. You're his friend."

Eddie clawed at his hair. "I heard they messed him up bad."

Bryan sat on the other side of Eddie. "Do you know why?" He fought to keep his voice calm and gentle, like Sarah's, so he wouldn't spook the man. "What were those men after?"

Eddie gnawed on a fingernail. "Crew wouldn't say. He just disappeared like five days ago. I didn't know if he was coming back, but then he showed up. He'd heard they came after you 'cause of him disappearing."

"Did he say anything else to you?"

Eddie stopped wiggling and pulling at his hair. "Only

one thing. He said 'if something happens to me, tell Sarah to go to the safe place.'"

Bryan glanced over at Sarah, who had gone completely white. "Eddie, you don't say a word of this to anyone."

Eddie put his finger to his lips. "It'll be our secret."

Bryan patted Eddie's shoulder. "That's right." He helped Sarah to her feet.

Concern etched across Sarah's face. "Eddie, why don't you use that phone to call your parents? Spend some time at home."

Eddie nodded and scratched his head.

As they walked back to the car, Sarah still had a stunned look on her face.

"You know what he's talking about, right?"

"The safe place is a cabin in the backwoods." Sarah opened the car door. "Crew and I ran away there when we were in a foster home that was less than wonderful. That must be where he took this woman." She climbed into the passenger seat.

Once behind the wheel, Bryan turned to face her. "You remember how to get there?"

She nodded. "I think I can find it. You can't access it by car. We'll have to drive up to the lake and then hike in four or five hours. I have some daypacks at my place and a hiking map."

"I don't know if it's safe to go back to your place."

"Who's to say he doesn't have men watching your place, too? Besides, you don't have a truck anymore that would make it up that mountain. My car is all-wheel drive." She crossed her arms. "And I need to check on my cat."

"Oh, yes, the cat." The level of care she showed for everything in her life made her even more endearing.

"Mr. Tiddlywinks is pretty independent, but he's been by himself for almost two days."

Bryan couldn't hide his amusement. "We'll go back to

your place for supplies, and to make sure your cat is okay. I don't want to waste much time. We need to get to that cabin to see if the woman is up there."

"You have an idea who the woman might be, right?"

Bryan let out a heavy breath. "We had a key witness disappear right before we were ready to take Mason to trial. Eva was the one person who could link Mason to the abuses that were happening."

Sarah sat back in the car seat. "You think it's her."

"Why else would Mason be so gung ho to get to her? He's overplayed his hand in a lot of ways. Sending his business partner to talk to you was kind of desperate."

Bryan drove Naomi's car across town, turning on the country road where Sarah lived. He saw no sign of a tail as he drove. Sarah's plan to switch out cars had worked.

"How is Naomi going to get her car back?"

"I'll call her," Sarah said. "She can bring your car out here and make the trade. I'll leave the keys in a place she can find them."

Her house came into view. Bryan pulled up into the driveway. The area around Sarah's house was flat and open. Not many places to hide. No cars were parked along the road.

"Looks okay," she said.

Bryan pushed open the car door. "All the same, we better check it out." His voice threaded with tension as his hand hovered over his gun.

FOURTEEN

They circled the entire house. The front door was unlocked just as she had left it on the day she'd run out of here. She pushed the door open and stepped inside.

Bryan peered over her shoulder.

Clearly the men had come back here after chasing them away.

Though the house wasn't in complete chaos, cupboards and drawers in the kitchen were open. Desk drawers, file cabinets, even her bookshelves with the photographs on it, had been disturbed.

She shuddered, unable to let go of the sense of violation. "Why?"

Bryan pressed close to her, placing a calming hand on her back. "They were on a mission to get Crew. Maybe they thought they could find some information that would help them."

A mournful meow came from the back of the house and a fat yellow cat appeared from around the corner. She swept the cat up and held him close. "Did you miss me?" She closed her eyes as he purred in her arms. "I know we don't have time to deal with this mess, but I have to at least make sure he has food and water."

Bryan nodded. "I understand."

After feeding the cat, Sarah grabbed two backpacks

from the closet, changed her clothes and found hiking boots. "These are daypacks. There's food and water, supplies for extreme weather conditions and a first-aid kit."

"We'd better get moving." His voice filled with a sense of urgency.

Once they were out of town, it took only minutes before they were on a forest road headed toward the lake. Bryan checked the rearview mirror several times, though he was fairly confident they hadn't been followed.

"So how old were you when you and Crew ran away to this place?"

She liked that he was curious. "I was twelve and Crew was fourteen. He stole a car. Things had gotten so bad with our foster care family at that time. We decided we would run somewhere nobody could find us."

"And so you came upon this forest service cabin?"

"We stayed up there for a couple of weeks. There were some canned goods already there and Crew was pretty good at catching rabbits and fish. We had a campfire every night, and we took turns reading from our favorite books. We called it the safe place because it felt like nothing in the world could hurt us there."

"So what happened?"

"A ranger found us. Crew wanted to run, but I knew we had to go back." Sarah bent her head. "They put us in a better foster home after that, but I think by then Crew figured he couldn't trust anyone but me."

"You know, the whole time we were dating you never told me any of that."

Sarah lifted her head. Was Bryan finally ready to talk about the past? "When you're sixteen, there's a lot of shame attached to not having a family. It was embarrassing enough that I was in foster care. I didn't share details with anyone. I wanted everyone to see me as a normal kid. I don't think your parents were very happy about their golden boy son dating the orphan even without me bringing up the unpleasant details."

His expression grew serious. "I wasn't very golden to you. I was kind of a jerk."

"It was a hard time for both of us." She looked away, not sure of what else to say, but feeling as though his admission had torn away at the protection around her heart. She toyed with the idea that there might be something between them again. How did he feel about her? Would he walk away after his case against Mason was wrapped up? The thought of being abandoned by him again doused the warm feelings she had for him. She had to know that he would stay with her no matter what.

The mountain road became more treacherous. Bryan focused on his driving.

Sarah studied the narrow, bumpy road. "There's no real parking lot. We're close enough now. You can pull off anyplace the road widens."

Bryan drove for a while longer until the trees to the side of the road thinned. Angling around the trees, he steered the car away from the road.

"I don't think we've been followed, but just in case, I don't want to take a chance that they find the car and disable it. Let's camouflage it, so it's not visible from the road."

They cut branches and picked some up from the forest floor. Satisfied, they headed through the forest after Sarah checked her compass.

"So this place must be hard to find," Bryan commented as they trekked up a steady incline.

"Forest rangers know about it. Crew and I stumbled on it."

"Have you been back there since that first time?"

"Couple Easters ago, Crew was doing pretty good. We went up there together."

They came out on the opposite side of the lake from where the thugs had initially brought Sarah. The fire tower, high on the mountain, was still visible.

The sun had sunk low in the sky when the cabin, nestled in a valley and surrounded by trees, came into view. A creek flowed not too far from the cabin, silvery in the waning light.

As they approached the cabin, Sarah saw no signs that anyone occupied it. Maybe that had been intentional on Crew's part.

"She's not going to be expecting us. She might be afraid," Bryan said.

"I think I know how to handle this." Sarah knocked on the door. "Hello, my name is Sarah. I'm Crew's sister. I've come to help you."

Bryan leaned toward the door. "Eva, if you're in there, this is Bryan Keyes. The policeman you talked to about Tyler Mason. We can protect you."

No response.

Sarah touched the door with her hand. "I know you're afraid."

The soft padding of careful footsteps reached her ears. Hope rising, Sarah glanced over at Bryan, who looked equally excited.

Without any warning, the door burst open, swinging outward and knocking Sarah to the ground. A woman with a tangle of wild blond hair ran out and bolted for the trees.

Sarah lay on her back with the wind knocked out of her. Bryan took off running after the woman. Still fighting for air, Sarah rolled over on her stomach and watched as Bryan caught the woman. He held her wrists while she screamed and kicked.

"We're not going to hurt you." He spoke in a soothing voice, but it didn't do any good.

She wrenched one hand free and slapped him across the

face. Sarah stumbled to her feet and ran toward them. "I'm Crew's sister." As Sarah drew closer, the woman gradually relented in her wrestling with Bryan. Clearly the woman was not the dark-haired Eva Bryan had described, but she looked familiar to Sarah.

"I'm going to let go of you. All right?" Bryan waited until the woman nodded. He released her wrists.

Breathless from her struggle, her shoulders moved up and down. She lifted the tangle of blond hair out of her face. Though she was rail-thin, intense blue eyes, high cheekbones and angular features made her a beautiful woman despite the malnutrition.

"I know you," said Sarah.

The woman nodded, relaxing a little.

"You came into my office six or seven months ago. You had a baby girl whom we helped you put up for adoption."

Understanding spread across the woman's face. "Crew said you help me. You did good for my baby." She spoke with a strong Russian accent.

"Nadia." Sarah touched the woman's cheek. "Your name is Nadia. I remember."

The woman glanced around nervously. "We go inside, please?"

They entered the cabin. A rolled-up sleeping bag with a pillow on top of it rested in a corner of the room beside a propane camp stove.

Nadia rubbed her stomach. "Crew supposed to bring me food days ago."

Sarah dug through her pack and pulled out a protein bar. She handed the food to Nadia. "Crew's in the hospital." She couldn't purge her voice of the emotion that statement brought up. "He's in critical condition."

Nadia's eyes widened. "Crew will be all right?"

"We think so," Bryan replied.

"Crew is a true friend." Nadia's entire body trembled as

she brought her hand up to her mouth. "He going help me get away for good, save some money. I need leave town." Desperation colored every word she spoke.

Bryan stepped toward her. "Maybe we can help—"

The boom of a rifle shot interrupted the conversation. The window by the cabin door shattered. Bryan pulled Nadia to the floor.

"Looks like they found us," Bryan said. His voice filled with indignation. "But how? I'm sure we weren't tailed."

Sarah hit the deck only a second after Bryan. She scrambled on all fours across the wooden planks. She waved Bryan and Nadia forward. "There's a back window in the other room."

A second shot tore through the thin wood of the door. Nadia screamed and covered her head with her hands.

Bryan tugged on her shirt. "We have to get out of here."

Nadia cried and murmured something in Russian as she shook her head.

Crouching below window level, Sarah returned. "Come on, Nadia, we have to go or they'll kill us for sure." Sarah grabbed the frightened woman's hand.

Still hysterical, Nadia complied.

"Stay low," Bryan commanded.

The window in the second room faced the back of the cabin. Nadia climbed through, then Sarah and Bryan.

The cabin door swung open on its hinges and banged against the wall just as Bryan's feet hit the ground.

It would take the shooter only seconds to figure out where they'd gone. They had to get out of the line of sight.

"This way." Bryan led them around to the side of the cabin and then toward the forest that would provide some cover. They were exposed for about twenty seconds.

Sarah hesitated, taking a moment to slip into her backpack. Bryan pulled Nadia toward the trees. Sarah ran twenty paces behind them. The first shot landed only a few feet behind her. Heart pounding, Sarah winced and then responded by running harder.

Bryan and Nadia reached the trees first. "Run," he shouted at Nadia and let go of her arm.

He sprinted back to Sarah and pulled her toward the trees, as well. The shooter stood in the open field a hundred yards away, lining up another shot.

Nadia ran about twenty yards into the trees and then stopped.

"Keep moving," Bryan shouted.

Nadia complied though she looked over her shoulder several times. They sprinted, jumping over logs, pushing branches out of the way. When ten minutes passed with no sign that the shooter had followed them, they slowed their pace.

Out of breath, Sarah studied the trees around her. "I'm all turned around. If we can get back to the lake, I can navigate from there."

"Not a chance. They'll be expecting us to do that. They'll be watching. I'm sure it's not only one guy after us." Bryan stuck his hands in his hair and stared at the sky. "What I can't figure out is how they found us. I'm sure no one followed us up here."

Sarah rolled her eyes. "So how do we get back to the car?"

Bryan turned one way and then the other. "We keep moving south. If we can find the road, we can find the car."

Sarah couldn't let go of the fear gripping her heart. Were they going to get out of here alive? "That could take hours."

"Going the obvious route could get us killed." His brisk walk turned into a jog. "Let's keep going."

Sarah increased her speed, as well. Nadia lagged behind. Her run turned into a walk and then she trudged. Sarah stopped and waited. "Do you want some water?"

Nadia nodded. She took the bottle and gulped. "Sorry,

I not so healthy. I have addiction problem for very long time. Just now getting strong."

"But you kicked it," said Sarah.

"I get away from my boyfriend, but he find me and he not so nice. He the reason I addicted in first place. Crew trying to help me get out of town."

Bryan, who had been listening from a distance, asked, "Nadia, what is your boyfriend's name?"

At first, Nadia took a step back. Her posture stiffened. Fear flashed in her eyes.

Bryan persisted, his voice growing softer. "Is his name Tyler Mason?"

She nodded.

A look of hard resolve materialized on Bryan's face. "So you got away, cleaned yourself up and found a place to live, but then he found you." Nadia nodded again.

The crackling of a branch caused them all to jump. Bryan put his finger over his mouth in a "be quiet" motion. Another breaking branch, this one closer. Bryan lowered himself to the ground and the two women followed.

Twigs and dried pine needles poked at Sarah's skin.

Nadia gulped and gasped. She squeezed her eyes shut. She wasn't handling this well, but who could blame her? The thought of Mason finding her obviously had her terrified. Nadia, more than Sarah or even Bryan, knew exactly what Mason was capable of.

Footsteps grew more distinctive as their pursuer crunched over the undergrowth.

Sarah reached over and placed a hand on Nadia's mouth. Her whole body vibrated with terror. *Please, God, don't let her scream and give all of us away.*

A fallen log shielded them on one side, but they would be exposed if the shooter passed by them to the west.

The footsteps continued. Judging from the sound, the

man was maybe twenty feet from them. Sarah held her breath. The footsteps stopped.

Nadia continued to shake as tears ran down her face. This was a woman who had been abused in her life. She gripped Sarah's hand and Sarah squeezed back, her heart going out to the woman.

Sarah had only visited with her briefly when she brought three-month-old April in for adoption. Nadia hadn't wavered at all in her decision to give the little girl up. Her determination to give her daughter a better life was admirable. Sarah understood that desire. She'd been through the same thing.

The footsteps, the crunching and breaking of under-growth, resumed. After what felt like a century, the sound of the shooter stalking through the woods faded altogether.

Bryan was the first to push himself up off his stomach. Still crouching, he turned a slow half circle, his hand wavering over his gun. He whispered, "Let's get going. Be as quiet as you can. Move as fast as you can."

Sarah helped Nadia to her feet. She wrapped an arm around her. "It's going to be all right. We'll get you to a safe place."

Nadia shook her head. "He will always find me. He found me here in the forest." Sarah picked up on the despair in Nadia's voice.

"Don't give up hope," Sarah said.

Nadia responded with a quivering smile.

They traversed down the hillside, being careful where they stepped, stopping to listen and watch. Bands of sunlight filtered through trees as the afternoon transitioned to evening.

After a while, without any disruption or indication that their pursuers were close, Bryan asked, "Why is Tyler so bent on finding you?"

Sarah could imagine the disappointment Bryan wrestled

with. He had thought they were making their way toward the woman who could tie up his investigation. Instead they had found fragile, wounded Nadia.

"He say it because he love me." A pained expression crossed Nadia's gaunt features. "But I don't think that is love. When I first came to America, he said I too pretty to work with the others who came with me. I thought I going to have the life, be a rich man's girlfriend."

Bryan slowed his pace and glanced over at Nadia. "You were one of the people he brought over here. And you know about the others?"

Nadia stuttered in her step. Her face went pale. She nodded for a long time before speaking. "I see some things."

"You've seen how he treats those people."

Again, the frightened young woman nodded.

Bryan stopped walking and turned to face her. "Nadia, I think there is a way to guarantee that he will never hurt you or anybody again."

"I do not believe it."

"He should go to jail for the things he's done."

"I wish that," said Nadia, her voice growing stronger, filling with bitterness.

"I think we can make it happen." Bryan touched her thin forearm. "First we have to get you in protective custody."

Heading downhill, they continued to walk through the forest.

Sarah's thoughts went back to the adoption she had arranged for the woman. Though she did not remember who Nadia had listed as the father of the baby, she did remember that there had been no objection from him. The adoption had been smooth in that way. The father had signed away rights easily. "Tyler made you give up the baby?"

Nadia shook her head. "He didn't love the baby. I knew I couldn't get away if I had April and I want her have something better. After adoption, it take months for me to find a way to escape. I have no money, no way to leave town." The whole time she talked, Nadia's voice trembled.

They heard the rumble of a car on the road long before a road came into view. Bryan lowered to a crouch and sought out a tree for cover. Sarah grabbed Nadia's hand and pulled her toward a tree not too far from Bryan. Nadia braced her back against the tree and stared at the sky.

Sarah peered around the tree to where a section of the rutty dirt road was visible.

"Looks like they're running patrols," Bryan whispered.

Sarah stared down the hill and at the surrounding landscape, none of which looked familiar. "How are we going to find the car?"

"I think if we stay this far back and walk parallel to the road, we'll run into it without getting caught."

Nadia glanced back up the hillside from where they had just come. She looked scared.

Fear danced across Sarah's nerves, as well. The shooter was still up there somewhere.

How many of Mason's men had followed them up here? Three? Four? At least one stalked through the forest behind them. And another drove a truck up and down the mountain road looking for them. They were being squeezed from both sides.

She wasn't sure if Bryan's plan would work. He probably had his own doubts. What other choice did they have though?

Bryan signaled for them to get moving. Sarah helped Nadia to her feet. The unfocused look in Nadia's eyes worried her. The young woman was fading away emotionally.

They walked parallel to the road, using the trees for cover.

Uphill, Sarah caught the glint of gunmetal in the fading light.

"Down." Bryan had seen it, too.

Now Nadia displayed a look of utter terror. She bolted free of Sarah's grip and out through the trees, running in a zigzag pattern. The first shot tore through a branch only inches from her .

Nadia let out a cry and kept running.

Did the shooter have a clear view or had Nadia's movement cued him in? Sarah resisted the urge to shout for Nadia to stop. It would only alert all their pursuers of their position. But it was too late for that caution now. She ran with Bryan at her heels.

Shortly afterward, Nadia stopped running and collapsed to the ground.

Up the hill, the shooter emerged from the trees, making a beeline toward Nadia.

"I'll hold him off." Bryan drew his gun.

The boom of the gunshot sounded behind Sarah. She dared not look back. She focused on getting to Nadia. She couldn't see the sniper anywhere. Had Bryan managed to drive him back?

Another shot shattered the silence. This one clearly from a rifle.

The gunshot caused Nadia to leap to her feet once more. Sarah grabbed at her shirttails. "Nadia, calm down. You have to be still."

Nadia flailed her arms. She cried with loud jerking sobs. Sarah wrapped her arms completely around her. "It's okay."

Gradually, Nadia's breathing slowed.

Bryan's footsteps pounded behind her.

His hand touched Sarah's back. "Let's keep moving."

"How? Where? We're sitting ducks here."

Bryan holstered his gun and pushed them toward a large tree that provided a degree of cover. He pointed downhill.

She could just make out the metal of the car beneath the camouflage of branches.

Bryan leaned close to her. "I say we make a run for it."

FIFTEEN

Though he could not see the shooter above them, Bryan assumed the man was making his way downhill and looking for an opportunity to line up a clean shot. They'd have about a hundred yards with no trees for cover. It was a risk, but they had no other choice.

They darted from tree to tree. Sarah took Nadia's hand and pulled her forward. At least Nadia wasn't crying or screaming anymore. He could not imagine what sort of trauma and abuse Mason had put the young woman through. He didn't want to imagine it.

In all his investigation, he'd never learned of Mason having a girlfriend, which meant that Nadia must have been a virtual prisoner. Would Bryan be able to set her free or would they all be captured?

They rushed toward the open grassy area. Bryan took up the rear. He faced uphill with his weapon drawn. A rifle shot rang out, stripping the bark off a tree not too far from him.

He glanced over his shoulder. Sarah and Nadia were feet away from the car. Now that he knew where the shooter was, he watched the trees and brush for movement. He saw a flash of white, fired off a shot and dashed behind a tree. He peered out, studying the forest. That should hold the shooter off and buy him the time he needed to get down the hill.

Down below, Sarah tore the last branch off the car. Bryan zigzagged down the hill, looking over his shoulder. When he no longer had tree cover, he bolted the remaining distance to the car.

Sarah left the driver's-side door open as she directed Nadia to the backseat.

A rifle shot sounded behind him, and when Bryan looked back, he saw the shooter barreling down the hill. Bryan increased his stride, leg muscles pumping. His hand reached out for the car door. His gaze traveled to his shoulder where a tiny red dot rested.

He ducked. The window in the driver's-side door shattered. Bryan crawled behind the steering wheel where Sarah had already put the key in the ignition.

Nadia screamed and cried from the backseat while Sarah sought to comfort her. Bryan turned the key in the ignition, shifted into Reverse and pressed the accelerator. He cranked the steering wheel and turned out onto the road. A Jeep appeared around a bend, heading straight toward them.

"Is it them?" Sarah asked from the backseat.

"We'll assume," said Bryan as he gritted his teeth.

The Jeep didn't stop or pull over. Bryan accelerated to a dangerous speed. His bumper collided with the bumper of the Jeep as he nudged it down the hill. At first, the driver pushed against the force of Bryan's car.

Bryan shifted into Reverse and backed up. The Jeep remained on the road, its engine rumbling.

They couldn't get around it. Not on this narrow section of road.

Bryan shifted into First and zoomed toward the other car. He meant to crash into them. The other car reversed.

The driver turned the wheel so the back end of the car slipped off the road.

Bryan squeezed past by directing his car partway up on the other side of the bank. It was working, but it was also a slow process, giving the shooter time to come after them from the woods. Several shots hit their back bumper.

Bryan increased his speed despite how hazardous the road was. The car shook and wobbled wildly.

"They must have shot out a tire." He gripped the steering wheel, willing the car to go further.

The car slowed and bumped along even though he pressed hard on the accelerator. He checked the rearview mirror. A pair of armed men were chasing after them, and gaining ground.

"We're going to have to run for it." He pulled toward the shoulder of the road. Down below was a grassy hill that led to the river. "Maybe it's better this way. I think they must have slapped a tracking device on your car. How else could they have found us? They must have been close enough to spot us hiking. Get out now. Head toward the river."

Sarah pushed open the door and grabbed Nadia's sleeve. Bryan took cover behind the driver's-side door and glanced up the hill. He searched the grassy hill for the two armed men. He looked on the other side of the road. A steep bank met with forest. One of the shooters darted stealthily through the forest. He saw a flash of blue, probably part of the pursuer's shirt, but even as he watched, the man lost his footing and tumbled downhill. A groan of pain came from the trees. Bryan turned his attention to the grassy hill below. Nadia bobbed in and out of sight between the low-growing junipers as she headed toward the river. He couldn't see Sarah.

He tensed. The second shooter headed down the hill toward Nadia. Nadia disappeared behind some brush, as did the shooter. An agonized scream filled the forest.

Bryan raced down the hill, his muscles straining. He searched the cluster of junipers where he had last seen Nadia. Where was Sarah? Fear enveloped him. Had he missed the sound of the shot? Did she lie bleeding in the grass?

The juniper trees shook.

Bryan lifted his gun, aiming at the tree. "You don't want to do this!" he called out.

The shooter stepped out from behind the gnarled trees. His arm was wrapped around Nadia's neck and he held the gun to her head with his free hand. "Yes, I want to do this."

From all the men who had come at them over the last few days, he didn't recognize this man.

"All I want is this woman," the thug said next. "So back off and I won't hurt you."

Bryan shook his head. He didn't believe that, not after all the times his cohorts had tried to kill him and Sarah for days. He lifted his gun and the man reacted by pressing his own gun harder against Nadia's temple.

Nadia made tiny gasping noises filled with intense distress. Her face was red. Her eyes filled with terror.

He needed to buy time, weaken the man's resolve. "What are you, the new hired muscle? Do you have any idea what your boss does?"

A flicker of emotion passed over the man's face. He opened his mouth to say something, but he didn't get a chance.

From behind the shooter, a large log rose up and slammed down on his head. Sarah appeared as the man crumpled to the ground.

"I hid when I saw him coming," Sarah explained. "Nadia wouldn't listen to me. She kept running."

On the hill above them, the man Bryan had watched fall paced the road, searching down below. He walked with a limp. The man on the ground in front of them moaned.

"We don't have much time." Bryan grabbed one of Nadia's hands and Sarah took the other one. They ran toward the cover of the cottonwoods that grew along the river. Nadia kept pace with them as they sprinted along the river.

Though it would be the fastest way back to civilization, following the river was too obvious. "Back into the trees," Bryan commanded.

The two women scrambled after him up the hillside. They jogged for some time until they came to a camp with a tent, a raft and fisherman's gear, but no person in sight.

Bryan searched the camp. "Hello?"

"I don't think anyone is here," said Sarah. She glanced nervously in the direction they had just run.

They both looked at the raft at the same time.

"We can get in touch with the owner via the forest service." He sprinted toward the raft. "Pay him back."

"Nadia, we need your help." Sarah grabbed a section of the rope that ran around the top of the raft. "Grab the paddles."

They ran for the river at a diagonal, putting more distance between them and their pursuers. The trees thinned and they crossed the rocky shore to the river. The water gushed and murmured as it slipped over the rocks.

Bryan glanced up the shoreline, but didn't see the gunmen. The sky transitioned from light gray to charcoal.

"I'll help you push out." Sarah stepped into the water. "Nadia, get in. Hold on to the oars."

Cool river water whirled around his legs as they pushed the raft toward the center of the river. The water was up to his waist by the time the raft gained momentum. Sarah placed her foot on the edge of the raft and Nadia helped her in. She scooted to the back of the raft and lifted Bryan in. The raft picked up speed as the river pulled them forward.

Bryan handed Sarah a paddle. "Now." In unison their

paddles sliced through the waves as the boat undulated over the top of the water.

"Let's work toward the opposite shore."

The water in this part of the river might be ten feet deep. Sarah touched Nadia's tangled blond hair. "Can you swim?"

Nadia shook her head.

They entered rougher water. The raft swayed more from the power of the rapids swirling around them. There was no sign of a gunman near them.

"We're losing air." Sarah's voice filled with panic.

They must have scraped against something sharp when they pushed it in the water.

Nadia let out a tiny gasp.

"Get to the shallow water," Bryan commanded as he paddled hard.

Water spilled over the collapsing side of the raft. It filled quickly. Sarah unzipped a pouch in her backpack and put something in her jacket pocket. She let go of the pack. Bryan had lost his when they'd abandoned the car.

Sarah grabbed Nadia's hand and wrapped it around the rope that bordered the rim of the collapsing raft.

"Hang on as long as you can. The shallow water isn't that far." She clutched both of Nadia's cheeks between her hands. "Can you do that for me?"

Nadia nodded.

"We'll stay as close as we can," Bryan said as he slipped into the water but held on to the raft rope. Sarah's back-pack floated away. The rapids chugged and swirled them around.

The force of the undertow suctioned around Bryan's legs. He had to let go of the raft so he could stay above water. He stroked toward the shore and watched as Sarah and Nadia floated farther downstream. They drifted around a bend out of sight. He felt solid earth beneath his feet. He stood up, splashing through the shallow water.

He ran along the shore hoping to see the two women in the fading light. He prayed he could get to them in time.

Nadia thrashed and grabbed at Sarah, pulled her under. Sarah gulped for air.

She's going to drown us both.

Only part of the raft was visible as it bobbed away from them. Nadia grabbed Sarah's arm. Sarah spoke between plunging underwater and rising to the surface. "Let go."

Nadia was like an anchor around her arm.

"Float, Nadia."

The weight lifted, but not because Nadia was floating. No, it was because she had let go. Nadia disappeared beneath the current. Sarah swam hard toward her. Her head bobbed to the surface and then she was sucked under again.

Oh, dear God, please no. Save her.

Sarah swam downstream, her muscles growing heavy and tired. Then in the light of the setting sun, Nadia's head surfaced.

She was too far away. She'd never get to her. Sarah dragged her arms through the water as hope sank. She had to at least try.

Water splashed downriver and off to the side. Bryan dove into the water and swam toward Nadia. She watched as he caught her and dragged her to shore.

Sarah swam to the bank and trudged toward the sound of the coughing and sputtering. She found Bryan kneeling next to Nadia, who lay on her side gasping for air and spitting up water.

"We made it." Sarah shivered. Aware now that the dropping temperature and being soaked to the bone was making her cold. "We have to build a fire."

"With what?" Bryan sat back, crossing his arms over his chest, probably trying to keep warm.

Sarah unzipped her coat pocket. "I grabbed the waterproof matches out of the pack before I let it float away."

Nadia sat up as well, her voice a little strained. "I'm cold."

Bryan craned his neck at his surroundings. "They might be searching the shoreline. A fire would make us an easy target."

"Let's hike back away from the river, see if we can locate a place that shelters us from view where we can make camp." Her voice vibrated from being chilled.

Bryan shook his head. "No camp. We have to find a way out of here before they catch up with us." He placed his hands on his hips, studying the darkening landscape.

"We can't move very fast if we don't get warmed up," Sarah countered.

Brian spoke slowly as though he were mulling over their choices. "Mason wants her back under his control… or worse. They've already shown that they're not going to give up easily."

Nadia's voice trembled. "Can't feel end of fingers."

Her comments brought home the gravity of what they were up against. "Twenty minutes by a fire sheltered from view and we'll be able to get out of here faster," Sarah pleaded.

Bryan didn't answer right away. His gaze fell on Nadia, who crossed her arms over her body and rocked back and forth. "Nadia, you stay here." He spoke to Sarah. "Move a hundred paces up the hill. I'll do the same downriver. If we don't find any place that would work to build a fire, we keep moving."

Sarah bolted up the hill. She and Bryan might be okay without stopping to sit by a fire, but Nadia wouldn't be. She'd been in rough shape physically and emotionally when they'd found her. She couldn't handle much more. She needed a break, and a few minutes to pull herself together. Unfortunately, Sarah wasn't doing very well finding a place suitable for that. The hillside was mostly brush and grass, nothing that could hide a fire from view.

She wondered, too, what the extent of Mason's manpower was. Once he'd been alerted to their location would he send more men besides the three they'd encountered?

A single word drifted across the night air. "Here."

She ran toward the sound of Bryan's voice. He emerged from the darkness. "Over there, rocks and a small cave. You start the fire. I'll get Nadia."

Sarah jogged up the hillside. An outcropping of boulders came into view. The flat rock jutted out from the side of the hill providing an overhang. The boulder in front of it blocked the view to the shoreline.

Sarah gathered kindling and a few larger logs from fallen trees and started the fire. Minutes later, she heard footsteps. Bryan slipped around the boulder, ushering Nadia forward. She gravitated to the fire.

"I kept it small," said Sarah. "Nadia, get as close as you can."

The tight space between the boulder and the overhang provided little room to move around as all three of them huddled close to the fire.

Nadia held her hand out toward the heat. Firelight flickered across her face. "Is it worth it?" she whispered.

"What do you mean?" Bryan squeezed in close beside Sarah, their shoulders touching.

"Maybe I go back to him. Give up." Despair colored her every word. "He will never stop." She let out a small cry. "And he hurt Crew."

"Nadia, don't say that. I know this is hard and hiding in that cabin was scary, but we'll get you out of here, and after that, the police will help you. They'll keep you safe," Sarah said.

Bryan shifted. "Nadia, you are the only one who can put him behind bars. And after he goes to jail, you won't have to be scared anymore."

In the flickering firelight, a tear drifted down Nadia's cheek. "I wanted my baby to be safe. He threaten hurt her if I do not do what he says."

Sarah cupped a hand on Nadia's shoulder. "And he doesn't have that power over you anymore. April is safe and happy."

Despite the tears, Nadia's voice held a lilt of joy. "I did a good thing for her."

"Yes, you did. He can't find her and he can't hurt her. All those records are sealed." Sarah stamped down a rising anxiety. She hoped that what she said was true. The reach of Mason's power surprised even her.

Bryan tugged on his T-shirt. "I'm starting to dry out."

"I warmer now," said Nadia.

Sarah stood up, looking for some way to douse the fire. She froze. Twenty yards away a flashlight beam bobbed in the darkness. Sarah's heartbeat quickened. The light came straight toward them.

SIXTEEN

Bryan jerked to his feet. Kicking dirt on the fire, he grabbed Nadia's shirtsleeve at the shoulder. "Come on, let's go. Run."

"Hold it right there," a voice boomed out of the darkness.

The nighttime had grown so quiet, Bryan heard the hammer on the pursuer's revolver click back.

"Put your hands up and step out, please, where I can see you."

Bryan couldn't quite process what was going on. The guy with the flashlight wasn't acting like one of Mason's henchmen. He sounded too…polite.

Both Nadia and Sarah stepped out away from the rocks.

"Is that all of you?" asked the voice in the darkness.

Bryan stepped out as well, squinting as the intense light shone on them. He could make out only the outline of a man behind the light.

"Are the three of you aware that campfires are illegal because of the high fire danger this time of year?"

Bryan laughed, relief spreading through him.

"Do you think this is a joke, son?"

Obviously, the ranger thought that they were teenagers out having some fun.

Bryan dropped his hand. "Sir, you have no idea how delighted we are to be busted for fire violations."

The ranger aimed the light directly on each of their faces. "Just what is going on here?"

Bryan stepped forward. "Sir, I'm a police officer with the Discovery P.D., and we need to get this woman into protective custody."

Bryan's explanation didn't seem to assuage the ranger's suspicions, so he tried another angle.

"I worked several weeks fire spotting. I'm a friend of Michael Duhurst."

The name-dropping must have finally won over the ranger. The defensiveness of his body language—shoulders back, chest out, gun pointed at them—melted. "Well, then, I guess I better get you down to my car and back to town. It's up over the ridge."

"You saw the fire from above?" Sarah sounded anxious.

The ranger pointed with his flashlight. "I patrol a road that runs along that ridge."

If the ranger saw the fire, someone else might have seen it, too. "Let's get to that car," Bryan urged.

They hiked up to the road. The ranger swung open the driver's-side door. "Don't mind Angie, she's friendly enough."

After Nadia climbed into the backseat, Bryan grabbed Sarah's damp sleeve. He glanced around the dark landscape. "If anything happens, you watch out for her."

Sarah nodded.

Angie turned out to be a black-and-white border collie, who settled in between Nadia and Sarah, alternating between licking the two women's faces.

The ranger turned around and grinned. "She likes people."

Bryan climbed into the front passenger seat. In the light of the car, he could see that the ranger was an older man, his gray hair cropped close to his head. Leathery skin spoke of years spent outside in the sun.

Bryan held out his hand for the ranger to shake. "Bryan Keyes."

"Daniel Monforton. Everybody calls me Ranger Dan."

The headlights cut a swath of illumination down the road. Bryan leaned back in the seat, still not willing to give up the idea that Mason's thugs would make another run at them.

In the backseat, Nadia laughed when Angie licked her fingers. She rested her forehead against the dog's and said something affectionate in Russian.

Sarah locked gazes with Bryan. She was probably thinking the same thing. How nice it was to hear Nadia laugh for the first time.

The ranger glanced toward the backseat. "She took to you like a fish to—"

The honking of the horn interrupted Daniel's sentence as his head fell forward onto the steering wheel. A sea of red spread out from Daniel's shoulder. The shot had come through so cleanly it left only a tiny hole in the driver's-side window.

The SUV veered off the road, rumbling down the hill. Nadia screamed from the backseat and Angie let out three quick barks. Adrenaline kicked through his body as Bryan grabbed the steering wheel. His feet fumbled to find the brake. The car rolled down the hill, gaining speed.

He brought the car to a stop.

Sarah leaned over from the backseat, placing her hands on Dan's neck. "He's still alive."

"Help me pull him over to the other seat." Though his voice remained calm, Bryan's heart raced. "Nadia, stay put and stay down."

The dog whined when Nadia let out a cry, but she did as she was told.

Bryan opened his door. He leaned in and wrapped his hands underneath Dan's armpits and pulled while Sarah pushed his legs out of the way. Dan moaned—conscious, but barely.

He glanced up the hill, speculating on where the shot had come from. Sarah climbed into the backseat and positioned herself so she could prop Dan up from behind.

Bryan cranked the wheel, easing upward toward the road. He switched off the headlights. "We're an easy target with them on."

"But we'll have to go so slow," Sarah said. "We need to get him to a hospital."

In the dark, he couldn't assess how badly Dan had been hit. The terrain hardened, indicating that they were back on the road. Bryan pushed the accelerator as hard as he dared. He checked the rearview mirror. Nothing. He could feel if they veered from the road when the SUV slanted at an angle. On the other side, the high embankment brushed against the side of the vehicle. Bryan gritted his teeth. He could do this.

Daniel stirred, expelling a pain-filled breath.

Sarah touched his head and made soothing noises. "He's still got a pulse," she whispered. "But it's getting weaker. I think he's lost a lot of blood."

Tension knotted through Bryan. The clock was ticking for Daniel, but if they all died, Daniel wouldn't have any chance of survival.

Angie let out a high-pitched whine. The sound of the tires rolling over the hard-packed dirt filled the car. Bryan stared out at the blackness in front of him.

He drove through the dark until he was satisfied that they were out of danger. He clicked on the headlights, increased his speed and headed out toward the main road. They encountered no other cars on the country road and only a few on the highway leading into town. Bryan zoomed up to the emergency entrance and pressed the brakes, stopping in front of the wide doors. Even before he came to a complete stop, Sarah pushed her door open and disappeared inside. She returned a few minutes later with two EMTs and a gurney. Dan's body was as lifeless as a rag doll when they loaded him onto the gurney.

"Nadia, come on, let's go inside."

Sarah ushered them into a waiting room while Bryan parked the car, then joined them inside. Bryan paced while Sarah stared down at the blood on her hands, Dan's blood.

"I wonder if he has any family."

"I can call Michael, the guy who got me the fire spotting job. Dan seemed to know him." Bryan took out his phone.

Sarah stood, as well. "I'm going to go check to see how Crew is doing."

Nadia lifted her eyes. "Crew is here?"

"Yeah, he's…he wasn't conscious when we were here earlier. I'll check and see how he's doing and come get you if he can have visitors," said Sarah.

"I like that very much," said Nadia.

Sarah trotted down the hallway and disappeared around a corner.

Bryan clicked through the contacts list on his phone until he found Michael's number. Once he got Michael on the line, he learned that Dan's wife had passed away and his only child lived out of state. Dan had a brother who lived in town, though.

"I think his name is Harry," said Michael. "I'll let the other rangers know. Dan is sort of the grandfather around here. He'll have lots of visitors tomorrow."

Bryan gripped the phone. *If he makes it.* "I'll see if his brother is listed in the phone book." Bryan said goodbye and hung up. He wandered through Admitting and another waiting area before he located a phone book. He found a listing for Harrison Monforton and made the call. Harry promised he'd be right up.

Bryan clicked off his phone and hurried back to see how Nadia was doing. When he entered the emergency room waiting area, Nadia was no longer in the chair where he had left her. Panic spread through him as he searched the area around the waiting room, still unable to find her.

The armed guard stood outside Crew's room as Sarah approached. When she walked up the hallway, a nurse raced into Crew's room. She was alone and she wasn't pushing a crash cart, but still, the drawn look on the nurse's face and her hurried step made Sarah's stomach do somersaults. Something wasn't right.

Sarah recognized the armed guard from the station.

"I'm Sarah Langston, Crew's sister. Do you remember me from the police station?"

He nodded. "Bryan's friend."

"Yeah." She glanced up and down the hall. "Have things been pretty quiet here?"

"No disruptions since they posted me."

In the room, Crew remained motionless and pale as the nurse bent over him.

"Has he woken up at all?" Sarah tensed, afraid of the answer.

The nurse shook her head and then glanced at the monitor by Crew's bed. "His heart rate and blood pressure have been dropping." She stood up straight, gripping the handrail and looking Sarah in the eye. "I have to be honest with you, none of this is a good sign."

"Can I sit with him for a moment?" Her throat tightened with emotion.

"Sure." The nurse left the room.

Sarah pulled a chair up. Crew's face could have been carved from stone...so lifeless.

She cleared her throat. "Hey, big brother, you have to pull out of this. 'Cause otherwise it just wouldn't be fair." She touched his cold cheek with the back of her hand. "You finally get your life together and then…" She sobbed. "And then it's taken from you because you tried to help Nadia, to do the right thing. You've gotta wake up," she whispered.

Sarah closed her eyes and prayed while she held Crew's ice-cold hand. When she was done, she stood up and slipped back into the hallway.

Bryan rounded the corner, his eyes wide with fear. "Did Nadia come this way?"

Sarah shook her head and then looked at the police officer. "Have you seen a blonde woman, pretty but thin?"

The officer shook his head.

Bryan balled his hands into fists. "I slipped around the corner to find a phone book. That was all." He turned back to the officer. "She's a material witness in a crucial case, and she's in a lot of danger. We've got to find her."

The officer pulled his radio off his utility belt. "I'll alert the other officer in the building. If she's in the area, we can find her."

"It's been five minutes, she's probably miles from here by now." Bryan's voice simmered with anger, threatening to explode.

"Let's not give up that easily. Some of the staff might have seen something through the glass, and I think Nadia would have put up a fight." Her words sounded upbeat, but Sarah feared they'd gone through so much only to lose Nadia to Mason.

As they ran through hospital corridors, Sarah wasn't sure if it would do any good to search. Bryan was right about Nadia likely being long gone by now. Both of them had let their guard down. She pushed through the waiting room. On the other side of the glass, a staff member stood hunched over a chart resting on the counter.

"Let's search the perimeter first and then question the staff, since time is everything now," Bryan suggested. They pushed the doors open; the cool night air surrounded them. She scanned the parking lot. A car wove through the rows looking for a parking space.

"I'll go this way," Sarah said. "We'll meet back here."

"Wait." He grabbed Sarah's sleeve and pointed. "Is that…"

The emergency room, hospital and doctors' offices formed a U-shape of connected buildings. On the opposite side of the U with the minimal light spilling from a distant lamppost, she could discern a person moving along the sidewalk.

Sarah squinted. Was that Nadia walking Angie on a leash?

Sarah took off running across the parking lot. "Nadia!"

Bryan ran behind her as the scene unfolded in slow motion. Nadia waved at them. The dog tugged her forward. The car she'd noticed earlier closed the distance on Nadia. Bryan ran faster, pushing past Sarah. Brakes squealed. A man jumped out from the passenger side, his hands reaching claw-like toward Nadia. Nadia screamed, pulling back as the man lunged at her on the sidewalk.

Sarah fought to keep up with Bryan as he sprinted across the lot.

Angie barked, jumping at the man. Nadia fell backward on the sidewalk. The assailant threw off the dog just as Bryan landed a hard punch against the man's jaw.

The car tires spun, burning rubber as it sped away. The assailant left behind fought back, raising his fist. Bryan blocked him and responded with a blow to the man's stomach, which bent him over. Behind him, the dog barked like a Gatling gun as Nadia held Angie's leash.

Bryan pulled his gun. "Stay right where you are. Hands behind your head."

"I'll call the police," Sarah said between breaths.

"Looks like your friend didn't want to stick around and help you out." Bryan jerked his head in the direction the car had sped away.

The man tightened his square jaw and sneered.

This was the first time they'd managed to detain one of Mason's hired thugs. Maybe after a couple of days in jail, Bryan could get him to share information about Tyler Mason.

"Nadia, why did you leave the hospital?" Sarah asked.

"I worry about dog." She wrapped her arms around the collie. "Can she stay with me? She protect me."

Sarah looked at Bryan.

Bryan shrugged. "I'm sure Dan's not going to be in any kind of shape to take care of her. If it's okay with his brother, it's fine with me."

The police sirens sounded in the distance.

Once the assailant was taken into custody, Sarah took Nadia in to see Crew while Bryan checked in on Dan.

Nadia's face fell when she saw Crew. She touched his forehead.

"Where did you two meet, anyway?"

"Rehab class. The only time Tyler not with me. He just friend, not romance." Nadia smoothed the blanket that covered Crew. "I want for him get better."

"Me, too." A lump formed in her throat. "I'll leave the two of you alone for a minute." She stepped out of the room and talked with the guard at the door for a few minutes.

Bryan stalked up the hallway. She ran up to meet him.

"Dan's going to be okay. He was even coherent enough to talk to me. He doesn't have a problem with the dog staying with Nadia. We need to get her out of here and into a safe house." He reached up and brushed Sarah's cheek lightly with the back of his hand. "Once we get something set up, you might want to think about staying there, too."

"How long? Until Mason goes to trial? Bryan, I have a job. I have a life."

"I can't keep you safe." Frustration was evident in his voice.

"I don't know if that's part of your job description." Sarah stared into his deep brown eyes. This was not the boy she had loved all those years ago. The kid who lost his sense of direction by trying to please everyone around him. Bryan had shown himself to be a man of integrity, willing to take on enormous responsibility. More than any man should have to carry on his own.

"It has nothing to do with the job." His fingers brushed over her cheeks and skimmed her lips.

If he kissed me now, I wouldn't pull away.

Bryan cleared his throat and looked behind him, aware of the officer in the hallway. The smolder in his eyes was enough to make her legs wobble.

"We better do what we need to do." His voice had a husky quality.

Nadia emerged from Crew's room, her eyes red from crying. They drove back to the police station. Bryan arranged for some food to be delivered and invited both women to rest on the couches in the police break room.

After they ate a meal of cheeseburgers and fries, Nadia settled down on a couch with Angie lying at her feet. Still a bit stirred up, Sarah closed her eyes but couldn't sleep. Bryan's desk was outside the break room; she could hear him making arrangements for a safe house for Nadia and for a lawyer to take her deposition. Slowly she drifted off to sleep. She awoke hours later with a blanket over her. Probably Bryan's doing.

She stretched, placing her bare feet on the cold linoleum floor. Nadia rested peacefully on her side. Angie had jumped up on the couch, snuggling between the back of the couch and Nadia's legs.

Sarah slipped into her shoes and peeked around the corner to where Bryan worked at a computer. He stopped when he heard her coming, lifting his fingers off the keyboard and turning to look at her.

"Hey." His eyes still held that same fiery essence she'd seen when they were at the hospital. "Sleep okay?"

She nodded.

He pushed a ziplock bag toward the edge of his desk. "One of the female officers put this together for you."

The bag contained a toothbrush and other toiletries. "Thank you."

"Oh, and these." He swung his chair around and picked up a pile of neatly folded clothing still with the price tags on them. "Officer O'Connor guessed at your size. There's a shower in the women's locker room."

Sarah stared down at the bag. For a moment, she felt a terrific rush of excitement at the thought of finally being clean, in fresh clothes. But then she caught herself. Was this her life now? She missed her own deep bathtub. She missed her cat and the quiet summer nights on her porch watching the sunset. She missed working at the adoption agency.

He must have picked up on her sadness. "We're hours away from setting up the safe house."

"Where is it?"

"In a little town about sixty miles from here. We've hired extra security. The background checks are still in progress. We want to make sure there's no way Mason can get to Nadia or to you. His network in Discovery is pretty extensive."

"I don't want to go." She looked into Bryan's rich brown eyes, realizing going to the safe house wasn't just about being cut off from her normal life. It also meant she wouldn't be with Bryan. The loss was like a hole blown through her heart.

"I know you don't want to stay locked away like this, but it might be our only option. It wouldn't be for all that long. Most of the legal case against Mason is already put together. Nadia's testimony is what we needed."

Sarah's throat went tight. Her heart pounded. She wanted to share her feelings, but the words wouldn't come. "Thank you for everything you've done…for Crew and for me."

He turned slightly away from her. "Family is everything."

She caught a tinge of bitterness in his voice. Was he thinking of the family he didn't have with her? Of the daughter they'd put up for adoption?

Sarah closed her eyes. She'd been foolish to think that they could take up where they'd left off. An unhealed wound would always exist between them, one that time couldn't fix. She couldn't bring their daughter back into their lives. Marie was with a family who loved her. They were her parents now. She couldn't reverse the events of ten years ago. If only they had gone slower, waited until they were married and settled. Things could have been so different.

"Guess I'll go take that shower."

Bryan focused on his computer screen. "Down the hall and to the right."

Sarah took a steaming hot shower, dried off and dressed. She combed out her wet hair and padded down the long hallway to the main part of the police station.

Bryan wasn't at his desk. Only two other officers worked at their computers. The clock said it was only 7:00 a.m. When she checked the break room, Nadia and Angie continued to doze.

Bryan came up behind her, touching her shoulder lightly. "Might want to wake her up."

"Where have you been?"

"In the interview room. That man who tried to grab Nadia at the hospital isn't giving up anything. He won't even admit that Mason hired him. It's entirely possible he's never met Mason. Second- or third-party associates could have hired him. Mason's really good at keeping his hands clean, but this has his fingerprints all over it."

Sarah gazed in at Nadia, who slept so peacefully. "Why do I need to wake her?"

"The safe house is ready."

Sarah's heart sank. "Guess this is it then."

She wouldn't be seeing Bryan Keyes anymore. She was out of excuses for being with him, and they couldn't seem to build a bridge over the chasm they had created ten years ago.

SEVENTEEN

Bryan deliberately didn't look at Sarah as she rode in the passenger seat while he drove the two women to the safe house. The sadness in her eyes stabbed at his heart. Over and over, his desire to hold her met him at every turn. The memory of the kisses they'd shared haunted him. But every time he looked in her eyes, all he felt was pain. The reality of them being separated drove the point home. As long as they were together, he could entertain the fantasy that they would be a couple again. The truth was the damage was too extensive. He'd failed his daughter. And then he had torn Sarah to pieces over that. He couldn't get past the self-condemnation. No matter how hard he tried or how much he wanted Sarah. He wanted to change the past and he couldn't do that.

"I think you will like the house," he said. They passed a sign indicating they had entered the small town of New Irish.

Sarah turned her head and stared out the window.

"The case against Mason can be assembled within a month. We'll be able to put him in jail even sooner. There's a huge flight risk because of his connections in other countries. No judge is going to grant bail."

Sarah smoothed over her shirt. "That doesn't mean

Mason won't stop giving orders to do us harm. I'm sure he'll find ways to get things done even from a jail cell."

He couldn't argue with her.

Nadia spoke from the backseat. "Will I be able to go outside with Angie?"

"There's a fenced backyard, and we have security people at the house all the time."

"But no running through the hills with the dog?" Disappointment colored her words.

"We don't want you to have too much exposure, and you can't go anywhere alone," Bryan explained. "The woman who lives at the house is a retired police officer. She'll provide your cover to the community, probably say you are her nieces or something."

"Not a lot of freedom," said Nadia. "But someday. I come to America for freedom. First I am Tyler's slave and then slave to drugs." Nadia's words sunk in deep, reminding him of why he wanted to take Tyler Mason down. He destroyed so many lives.

They pulled up to a blue house with a chain-link fence and blooming flower beds. A woman with silver hair cut in a bob walked down the steps to greet them. "Hello, I'm Evelyn." She ushered the women in. Angie stayed close to Nadia, wagging her plumagelike tail. "Why don't the three, or rather, four—" she smiled down at Angie "—of you come in and I'll show you around."

Bryan followed them inside to where a tall man with a buzz cut and high cheekbones sat at a table. The man stood up, revealing the gun on his belt. He held out his hand. "Jason Smith from Firelight Security."

Bryan shook his hand. He had a vague memory of looking over Jason's profile before sending it to another officer for a deeper background check. Firelight had a solid reputation for security. The department could not afford to lose officers for the 24/7 watch Nadia required.

Nadia's exclamations over features in the house floated in from another room. Sarah slipped out into the backyard. Bryan followed her. Her hair shone in the sunlight. How many times had he buried his face in that hair, enveloped by the soft floral scent? Her shoulders were slumped. All of her body language communicated sadness.

"I'll get one of the other officers to bring some things from your house if you want to make a list."

"We went there once to get the backpacks. Everything was okay. Why can't I get my own things?"

"Sarah, we need to think in terms of high security here. Not take any chances. We've come this far. You can have your stuff, just let us be the ones to get it for you."

"And my cat? Someone will bring Mr. Tiddlywinks?"

He smiled. "And your cat."

She turned to face him. "I know this has to happen. I see how badly Mason wants to take me out of the equation along with Crew and Nadia." She crossed her arms over her chest. "I just don't like it."

He descended the steps. "Wish it could be some other way." From the moment he'd climbed in the car to bring her here, an ache had entered his heart. Being away from her would be torture.

"I know you're doing the best you can." She touched his jaw with the softness of a feather and then leaned in and kissed his cheek.

He wrapped his arm around her waist and pulled her close. His lips covered hers. He kissed her for the beautiful memories they shared, not the ugly ones. He pressed harder, kissing her for what might have been. He rested his palm against her neck, holding her close, not wanting to let go. "I'm sorry." He kissed her again. "I'm so sorry."

She wrapped her arms around him and hugged him.

He pulled away. "I have to go." He turned, knowing that looking back at her would rip him to pieces. He said goodbye to Jason Smith, who still sat at the table. Bryan stepped across the threshold of the front door.

He climbed into the police vehicle and zoomed toward the road. What tore him up more than anything was that he wanted to be the one to stay with Sarah, to keep her safe rather than leaving her in the care of some stranger. He hadn't protected her heart all those years ago. Maybe if he could make up for it then the ache inside would go away.

His cell phone rang.

"Yeah." Bryan pulled over on a shoulder.

"Bryan." He recognized Officer Grant Pittman's voice. "I know we're done with the background checks for the safe house, but I found something when I did a little digging."

"What did you find?"

"It's not a big thing, but you said to flag anything that didn't feel right. I didn't catch it on the first pass 'cause it's not what you'd normally look for. But I read over the resumes of the guys we hired from Firelight and something caught my eye."

"One of them worked through Mason's temp agency?" Certainly they would have flagged something like that.

"No, not that tight a connection. I started doing some cross-referencing and turns out one of them used to live in Spokane and work for a restaurant Mason owned."

Bryan tensed. "Which guy are we talking about?"

Grant's reply was like a sword through Bryan's chest. "Jason Smith."

Angie's intense barking alerted Sarah to trouble inside the house. She ran up the stairs from the backyard, flinging the door open. The living room was empty. Persistent barking and scratching led her to the downstairs bathroom where Angie had been shut away.

The dog burst into the living room, sniffing the furniture frantically and darting back and forth. Sarah ran into the kitchen and peered out the window. Nobody was in the front yard. She sprinted halfway up the stairs. "Hello, Nadia? Jason? Evelyn?"

Silence.

She bolted the rest of the way up the stairs, searching the first bedroom and bathroom. In the second bedroom, Evelyn lay on the floor, unconscious but breathing. A heavy weight pressed on Sarah's chest, making it hard to breathe. What exactly was going on here?

Sarah fell to her knees as fear spread through every fiber of her being. "Evelyn, can you hear me?"

Evelyn's eyes fluttered open. "Hit from behind," she mumbled.

Evelyn didn't seem to be hurt anywhere else. No cuts, no bleeding. Sarah grabbed a pillow from the bed and placed it underneath Evelyn's head. "Just lie here, I'll figure out what's happened." She noticed Evelyn's gun in a holster and belt draped over a chair. She pulled the gun out and placed it in the older woman's hand. "Just in case."

Sarah hurried downstairs and out onto the front porch. She ran to the edge of the yard. A small compact car still sat in the driveway, as did the larger black truck. Nobody had left the house in a vehicle, anyway. She pulled her phone out of her pocket to call Bryan.

Bryan's car roared up the road. He braked and rolled down the window. "Where's Nadia?"

Sarah shook her head. "I'm not sure. I think—the cars are still here, but I don't see any sign of Nadia. Evelyn was knocked out. They must have got to Jason, too."

Bryan turned off the engine and jumped out of the car. He grabbed Sarah by the elbow and headed toward the front door, glancing in one direction and then the other. "They're not in the house?"

"Not that I can find."

He pulled her inside.

"Evelyn is upstairs," she whispered. "She'll be okay."

He pressed against the wall. "Stay close to me."

"What's going on here?"

"Jason is in on this," he said. He put his finger across his mouth, indicating she needed to be quiet. He raised his head to the second floor, listening. His hand wavered over his gun. Only silence.

Angie barked from a room off to the side. Bryan pulled Sarah in that direction. The room contained a washer and dryer and a wall where coats were hung. Angie scratched at the outside door.

Sarah shrugged. "They couldn't have gone out the back door. I was in the backyard. They didn't go out the front. I would have seen them going up the street. They had to have gone out this side door."

He eased the door open, peered outside and ducked back in. "There's a field out there and beyond that a barn."

"You think that's where they went? Why not just jump in the car and escape with Nadia?"

"Maybe you interrupted him when you came in from the backyard."

She clutched his shirtsleeve. "We need to call for help."

"We don't have that kind of time." His finger trailed over her cheek and across her lips. "You stay here. I'm going to see if I can sneak up on him."

"No, you can't go. That's too dangerous."

"Sometimes you don't have a choice." He kissed her full on the lips.

The intensity of his kiss burned her to the core as he pulled her back into the living room. "We'll get a better look at the barn from here." He pointed toward the window.

A shot boomed through the air, shattering the window. He jumped on top of her, taking her to the floor.

Stunned and trembling with terror, Sarah lay on her stomach. Angie barked and tugged on Sarah's shirt.

"That's where they are. Jason has sniper training. Maybe he gets a bonus if he takes us out, too." He crawled toward the front door. "Pull those drapes."

Avoiding the shards of glass, Sarah crouched and moved across the floor, shutting all the curtains. Bryan slipped out the front door. He'd have been a sitting duck if he'd gone out the back door where the sniper would've seen him coming.

She pulled herself up just above the windowsill and peeked out. Bryan had circled around to the back of the house. As she watched, he dove down and crawled through the tall grass toward the barn. No more shots were fired. The sniper hadn't seen him.

Sarah took in a deep breath that did nothing to calm her nerves. She felt helpless. She couldn't just sit here. Bryan could die. She needed to help him somehow.

Thudding noises came from the second floor. Sarah met Evelyn as she careened down the stairs. She held her gun. "I saw from the window. There's two of them. One is still up in the barn and the other is headed in this direction." Evelyn lifted up the gun. "Do you know how to use one of these?" Still unsteady on her feet, Evelyn swayed.

She'd gone hunting with Crew and with Bryan when they'd dated. She didn't really know if she could shoot at a person…but maybe the bad guys wouldn't realize that. "Yes, I think I can remember."

"Get the car." Evelyn handed her the gun. "Take the road that loops around to the back of the barn. They won't see you coming. I'll cover you and Bryan from the attic window with my husband's rifle."

Sarah sprinted out to the car, hopped in and drove. Instead of taking the fork that led back out of town, she turned onto a dirt road. The car was an electric one that didn't make much noise. She'd be able to get pretty close without being detected. Off to the side, she could see the top of the barn. A rolling hill shielded the rest of the structure from view.

She prayed for strength and courage.

Two shots in rapid succession boomed through the air. Sarah cringed and gripped the steering wheel tighter.

EIGHTEEN

Bryan ducked down in the tall grass. A shot whizzed past him and another traveled over his head toward the barn. He stared back at the house, unable to discern anything. Was Sarah shooting from a high window?

He lifted his head. In the exposed door of the barn loft, he caught a flash of motion. Then he heard it—the swishing sound of someone moving through the tall grass.

Two men? Bryan pressed his stomach hard against the ground and listened. Wind rustled through the grass.

He sensed eyes on him.

Heart raging in his chest, Bryan flipped over, scanning everywhere, aiming his gun—right, middle, left. Someone was here…close.

Still unable to shake the feeling of being watched, he dragged himself forward in the grass. His belly scraped over hard dirt and pebbles. Three feet from him, he spied drops of blood.

A hand grabbed the back of his collar, pulling him upward and choking him. Bryan flipped over and managed a boot to the man's knee. The assailant released only a small grunt of pain before he swiped Bryan hard against the jaw with the butt of a rifle.

The blow to his face stunned Bryan, made his eyes water. He rolled to one side as the man came after him again, realizing a moment later that he'd dropped his gun. When Bryan reached for it, the man crushed his fingers with his boot.

Bryan craned his neck. One of the man's hands was bloody, the fingers curled in at unnatural angles. Somebody had gotten off a good shot. With his hand still anchored to the ground by a boot, Bryan swung his legs and hit the man in the back of the knees. The assailant buckled to the ground. Bryan stood up, landing a hard blow to the man's head. A shot whizzed through the air. Bryan hit the deck. Another shot from the other direction stirred up dirt not too far from Bryan's head. He was in the middle of a firefight.

The man who had attacked him fell onto the ground face-first, not moving but not dead. The bullet hadn't hit him. The blow Bryan had given him knocked him out. Bryan grabbed the man's rifle and scampered through the grass. When he lifted his head, he detected no movement by the loft door. He'd be exposed the remaining distance to the barn, but he'd have to take his chances. He was running out of time before Jason Smith gave up and just took Nadia. He pushed himself to his feet and sprinted toward the barn.

A rifle shot exploded the air around him and then another.

From the back side of the barn, Sarah heard the volley of shots, cringing each time. She eased the car toward a small door, slipped out and pressed the barn door open. The door squeaked on its hinges. Sarah held back, her heart pounding in her chest.

After a moment, still in a crouch, she peeked into the building. Footsteps pounded across the loft. The scent of hay and manure hung in the air, though it looked like the barn hadn't been used in some time.

The lower half of the barn consisted of a series of stalls. She started checking them, but found no one. Nadia must be up in the loft with Jason Smith.

Sarah pressed against the rough wood of the stall. What could she do to get Nadia away from the shooter? Maybe she could create a distraction that would bring him to the edge of the loft so she could shoot him. Then she could climb the ladder and get Nadia. They'd have to jump from the loft to the ground outside to avoid Jason.

She looked around for something to make noise with. When her search brought her to the next stall, she stopped. Nadia sat hunched over in a corner, her hands and feet bound, a gag in her mouth.

Sarah ran over to her. She picked up a nail from the barn floor and cut Nadia free. "Quiet," she whispered. She grabbed Nadia's hand. Looking over her shoulder, she wove in and out of the stalls. The stomping of the shooter stopped. Had Bryan been able to disable him? They slipped through the door as a rifle shot splintered the wood above them.

She could hear Jason shouting expletives as she and Nadia raced back to the car. Sarah started the car. She glanced out at the road and then at the field that lay between the barn and the house. She had a choice to make. She knew she was supposed to get Nadia out of there, but she couldn't leave Bryan behind.

She hit the gas and zoomed out into the field. Bryan stood in the middle of the field aiming a rifle at the barn. She accelerated toward him. Without a moment's hesitation, he jumped into the backseat. "I think I got him when he ran around the side of the barn after you two."

The car slowed through the taller grass.

"This isn't an off-road vehicle." Bryan's voice held a note of humor.

"We'll make it." Sarah pressed harder on the accelerator.

Bryan glanced over his shoulder. Jason was halfway across the field. He favored his left leg. That must be where he'd hit him.

The car slowed to a crawl.

Bryan yanked open the door to tug Nadia out of the car. "Run," he commanded.

All three of them crouched low and sprinted toward the backyard. Angie burst out of the open door, meeting them at the gate.

Evelyn peeked her head out. "Hurry, get inside. Help is on the way from Discovery. We've only got one policeman in New Irish and I don't think he would be of much use."

Sarah and Nadia collapsed on the floor, exhausted and out of breath. Bryan darted over to a window, pulling a curtain back and peering out. He bent over, gripping his shoulder.

Sarah scrambled over to him. "You're hurt."

"Just a nick." He grimaced.

Evelyn stepped across the floor holding her rifle. "I can watch the field."

Bryan leaned against the wall. Sweat beaded his forehead. Sarah peeled back his bloody shirt. She sucked air through her teeth. "That's quite a gouge." She touched the skin around the wound and he winced. "I don't think the bullet went in."

"First-aid kit in the bathroom," Evelyn said without taking her eyes off the window.

Nadia jumped to her feet and headed toward the bathroom. She returned a moment later and slid the kit across the floor to Sarah.

"I think our guy has given up," said Evelyn.

"They don't give up." Bryan spoke through gritted teeth.

Evelyn scooted along the window. "I can't see him anywhere."

Sarah placed disinfectant on Bryan's torn, bloody skin.

She stared down at the kit. There wasn't a bandage big enough to cover the cut. She grabbed some gauze and placed it gently over the cut.

Gratitude shone in his eyes. He winked at her. "Thanks for saving my bacon."

She touched his cheek. "Thanks for saving mine."

Outside, sirens sounded in the distance.

The tightness of Bryan's expression told her he was still in pain. "Looks like the cavalry is here."

She put out a hand to help him to his feet. The four of them trudged toward the front door as the police sirens grew louder.

A single thudding noise came from the side entrance. Jason Smith appeared, the rifle aimed at Sarah as she stepped toward the front door. Bryan pushed her out of the way. The boom of a rifle blast contained within the four walls of a house echoed in her ears as Jason tumbled to the floor, still alive but in pain.

Evelyn let the arm that held the rifle she'd just fired fall limp at her side. "You said they don't give up, so I was ready."

Discovery police officers burst through the door ready to shoot. They escorted Nadia and Sarah out while Bryan briefed them on what had happened. After receiving first aid, Jason was taken into custody.

Sarah sat in the back of the police car with Nadia and Angie. She craned her neck to see Bryan coming out on the porch. As the police car pulled out of the driveway, Sarah wondered if there was any hiding place where Tyler Mason wouldn't find them.

NINETEEN

Bryan placed the phone in the cradle and studied the two weary women in front of him. They'd been brought directly to the police station from the safe house. "We've made arrangements for you to stay at a hotel for the night."

"Just for one night?" Dark circles had formed under Sarah's eyes. Nadia didn't look much better.

"We can't risk him finding out where you are. Our best option right now is to move you often." Bryan glanced around the police station. This time of day, most of the officers were out on patrol. The other detective had left to do an interview on another case. Only two other officers sat at their desks.

Bryan stood up and rested an arm on one of the walls of the carrels. He addressed his comment to Grant, who sat at his desk staring at his computer. "Quiet day, huh?"

"Compared to yours," said Grant, running his hands over his short buzz-cut hair. "We did have a break-in at the 2100 block on Oak Street."

"What business on Oak Street?" Sarah had come up behind him. Her voice sounded strained.

Grant sat up a little straighter in his chair and tilted his head. "That adoption agency downtown. Why?"

"That's where I work." When she turned to look at him, her face was whiter than porcelain. Fear danced across her eyes.

Bryan pieced a picture together. This wasn't a coincidence. "They searched your home. And now your workplace…."

Sarah thought for a moment. "There would have been pay stubs, letters in drawers." She turned away. "There's even a magnet on my refrigerator that says where I work."

"They put two and two together and figured out you might have something to do with April's adoption."

Nadia released an audible breath. "No." She jumped to her feet, shaking her head and pacing, her voice growing more and more frantic. "He will use the child to get my silence. He never loved the baby."

Sarah ran over to Nadia, grabbing her hands at the wrists. "He won't find what he's looking for. Those records are sealed in computer files. There are passwords and other security measures."

Tension melted from Nadia's body. "If you say." Sarah let go of her wrists.

Bryan walked over to Grant. "Can you keep an eye on those two? And I think the dog will need to go out for a walk. The women are not to leave the building."

"I'm stuck at my desk for at least two more hours. I can do that," said Grant.

Sarah ran over to Bryan. "Where are you going?"

"Out to see the extent of the damage at the robbery," he said.

"I'm going with you." Sarah touched his sleeve. He saw the look of hard resolve in her eyes. "I'll be able to tell you if any information on the computers has been compromised."

The truth was he didn't want to leave her anywhere and risk losing her again. "All right, but don't get out of my sight." Bryan stalked over to Nadia. "You stay here. Don't even go outside to take a breath. Do you understand me?"

Nadia nodded.

"Officer Pittman will deal with the dog."

Nadia lifted her chin. "I stay here."

"We'll get you moved to that hotel in a couple of hours."

Nadia slumped back down, her expression indicating that she understood. "Don't let him get April." Fear and desperation clouded her eyes.

Bryan drove Sarah toward the robbery location.

Sarah laced her fingers together as the city streets passed by. "Would he really go after the baby?"

"Maybe," Bryan said. "He's getting desperate. He can't get at Nadia directly. He's tried."

Bryan slowed the car as they came to a large brick building that housed several offices. Patrol officers had already cordoned off the place.

"Let's go inside." He pushed open his door.

Sarah led the way up the sidewalk. Bryan stopped one of the techs working the scene. He placed his hand on the small of Sarah's back. "We need to go inside. She works here. She'll know what's been taken."

The tech wiped the sweat from his forehead. "Pretty obvious what they stole. After they rooted through a bunch of file cabinets, they pulled all the hard drives from the computers."

Sarah seemed to collapse, her shoulders slumped and her head bent. "He's trying to find out who April's adoptive parents are."

Adrenaline coursed through Bryan's body. The break-in had taken place hours ago. How long would it take Mason to find what he was looking for? With all the men he had on his payroll, there was bound to be a computer expert or two who could get past the security measures. "We can call the parents, warn them."

"I don't remember their phone number. All that information is private. It was on the hard drives. I doubt they are listed in the phone book. They only have cell phones. And I'm sure I deleted them from my contacts list ages ago."

"Can you disclose where the adoptive parents live… for April's safety? We can dispatch an officer to check on them."

"They live out in the country. I took April out to them for visits several times. It would be faster for us to go there," said Sarah. "Besides, I feel responsible here."

"Then let's go. I'll alert the station as to what is going on."

She grabbed his hand. "What if Nadia hears the radio? She does not need any more turmoil. We don't want her doing something crazy."

"I can't go maverick on this." He turned a half circle and looked up at the sky. "I can phone it to the chief, though. Nothing for Nadia to overhear." The concession was worth it for Sarah's grateful smile.

Once they were out of town, Sarah directed him along country roads. The car crested over a hill, and a cabin at the base of a heavily forested mountain came into view. A car stood in the driveway. Nothing appeared amiss. Bryan pulled up close to the front door.

Sarah led the way up the front porch stairs. She knocked on the door. "Her name is Mackenzie and his name is Christopher. They're a neat couple. April is the second child they've adopted. The other is a four-year-old autistic boy named Ethan." Her words held a warm glow.

"You like your work?"

She gazed at him, blue eyes shining. "It's rewarding."

"Did you do it because of Marie?" It was the first time he'd spoken their child's name. He'd feared that all the pain of their bad choices would come rushing back with that single word. Instead, he felt a sense of release. Something that had been in the darkness, that he had refused to think about, was brought into the light.

She studied him for a moment. "Not entirely. I wanted to do a job like this because Crew and I languished so long in the foster care system. Things might have turned out better for Crew if someone had cared a little more about finding us a permanent family. I didn't want another kid to have to go through that."

"I think what you do is a good thing, a noble thing."

Happiness at his admiration shone in her eyes. "Thanks."

Bryan leaned in and knocked on the door a second time.

"Someone must be here. There're two cars in the driveway." Her voice had a nervous edge to it.

Bryan walked around the house. No one was in the backyard. Sarah met him on his way back. "The door isn't locked. I think we should go inside and take a look."

He pushed the door open and stepped across the threshold. A fan whirred on the high ceiling of the cabin.

"Mackenzie?" Sarah took several steps into the living room. "Christopher?" She walked toward the kitchen. "Ethan?" With each name, her voice became more filled with anxiety.

Bryan's hand hovered over his gun. "I'll search upstairs." He didn't want to leave Sarah alone. They'd been blindsided too many times. "Why don't you come with me?"

They moved silently up the carpeted stairs and down the hallway.

"Mackenzie? It's Sarah from the Loving Hearts adoption agency."

They searched all the bedrooms. The house was empty, silent. Bryan stopped in front of what was probably a bathroom. His back stiffened. "This is the only door that is closed." He adjusted his grip on the gun.

Sarah pushed the door open. Bryan slipped inside, scanning the room. The shower curtain shook. Someone was in the bathtub. He kept his gun aimed at the trembling curtain and signaled to Sarah that she should pull it back.

A woman with a gag on her mouth and fear in her eyes reeled back from Bryan pointing the gun on her.

"Mackenzie." Sarah bent toward the woman and peeled off the gag.

Bryan holstered his gun.

Mackenzie let out a burst of air once the gag was off. "The children. They took the children."

Sarah worked to untie Mackenzie's hands. "We think they only came for April."

Fear clouded each word Mackenzie spoke. "Then where's Ethan?"

"He wasn't in the house that we could find." Bryan struggled to keep his voice steady. Would they hurt an innocent child?

"He may have hidden. When he hears a stranger's voice, it scares him." Mackenzie leaned forward to untie her feet. She grabbed Sarah's shirtsleeve. "Why do they want April? Do you think she's all right?"

Sarah patted Mackenzie's arm. "She will be. We'll find her. Right now, why don't you focus on figuring out where Ethan went?"

Bryan leaned toward the woman. "Can you tell us what the men looked like?"

"They were wearing masks. There were three of them." She stepped out of the bathtub and ran down the hall calling Ethan's name.

Bryan and Sarah chased after her down the stairs. She emerged from one of the side rooms on the first floor. "Ethan isn't in his usual hiding place." She ran one direction and then the other. "I have to call Chris."

Bryan understood Mackenzie's panic, but he needed information. "Can you tell us which way the men went?"

Mackenzie stopped. Her eyes glazed as a confused look

came across her face. "We were upstairs and they came barging in. They took her from my arms. It happened so fast. The man knew April's name." A veil seemed to drop over her eyes as her voice grew cold. "He said 'come to Daddy' and he took her."

TWENTY

Sarah let what Mackenzie had said sink in. So Mason had felt this mission was so important, he'd taken care of it himself. Or maybe he was running out of hired guns to do his dirty work for him.

Bryan jumped into action. "We've got to get search parties out in every direction. They couldn't have gotten far." He turned back to face the frightened mom. "How long ago were they here?"

Mackenzie rubbed her temple and squeezed her eyes shut. "Ah…I was…tied up and left there maybe ten or fifteen minutes before you guys showed up."

Bryan nodded and pulled his phone out.

Sarah wrapped her arm around Mackenzie. "Let's focus on finding Ethan. Is there another place he would hide if he were afraid?"

"The thing is…he'd come out if he heard my voice," Mackenzie said.

Sarah fought hard to remain calm. Mackenzie didn't need to see the fear that pressed on her from all sides. "How about the backyard? He couldn't hear you from inside the house. Is there a place for him to hide outside?"

Realization spread across Mackenzie's face. Her voice had a haunted quality. "What if he ran after his sister? He's very protective of her."

The thought of a four-year-old boy lost in the forest, chasing after dangerous men, sent chills through Sarah. In the next room, Sarah could hear Bryan making frantic calls to get a search underway.

Mackenzie crossed her arms over her body. "I have to call Chris." She muttered something under her breath and stepped into another room.

Bryan emerged with his phone in his hand. "I've asked for law enforcement and search-and-rescue to find these guys…and the little boy."

Sarah felt numb all over as fog invaded her brain. "She thinks the boy may have gone after his sister."

Bryan kicked the leg of a chair. "This is bad. How could anyone put a kid in jeopardy like that?"

"As soon as Mackenzie calls her husband, we'll go out. We'll start calling for Ethan. He couldn't have gotten far." If something didn't get him first. The forest was crawling with bobcats and bears—and men like Tyler Mason.

Bryan's phone rang again. She watched his expression harden as he listened and then answered by saying, "Well, get her over there as fast as you can." He clicked the phone off.

Sarah stepped toward him. "What is it?"

Bryan's hands curled into a fist. He ran his fingers through his hair. His expression grew grimmer as he closed his eyes and tapped his forehead with his fingers. "Mason knows we're keeping Nadia at the station. One of his thugs got her on a phone and let her listen to April cry. Nadia fell apart and tried to leave the station. She'd do anything to make sure that baby is okay including trading herself for the baby's safety."

Sarah swallowed as her throat grew tight. Mason was pulling out all the stops. "I assume the other officers are watching her closely so she can't leave the station."

"They're taking her to the hotel room right now. We'll

have two officers with her at all times. She'll be shielded from Mason's destructive influence for a while anyway." Bryan took in a heavy breath. "One good thing. We have a better idea of where Mason is. We can pinpoint which cell tower provided the signal for his phone call."

Mackenzie emerged from a side room, her eyes red from crying. "Chris is on his way here from work."

"There will be search teams all over here in less than thirty minutes. In the meantime, we can cover the area in a wider and wider circle calling out for Ethan. It won't do any good for me to go alone if he only responds to your voice," Bryan said.

Though she still looked like she was in shock, Mackenzie nodded.

"I'll go with you, too," said Sarah.

They circled the yard and then outside the yard. Mackenzie called Ethan's name over and over, her voice growing weaker. A helicopter soared overhead. Probably part of the search team.

"What was your son wearing?"

"A yellow shirt and orange shorts." Mackenzie rubbed her neck, her voice filled with anguish. "Those are his favorite colors."

Bryan glanced up and down the road "Did you hear a car pull up or the sound of one leaving?"

Mackenzie's hand fluttered to her chest. She bit her lower lip. "It all happened so fast." She stared up at the sky, probably trying to piece the horrible memory together. "Come to think of it, I didn't hear a car. It's quiet out here. The horses make a lot of noise when someone shows up."

With the two women following him, Bryan stalked around to the side of the house circling a corral confining two horses. "That means they parked some distance away so they wouldn't be noticed." He continued to survey the area surrounding the house, pointing to the forest that jutted up against the backyard. "What's on the other side of those trees?"

"There's an old logging road," Mackenzie said.

Bryan picked up his pace. "Let's look for your son through there."

Mackenzie trotted toward the forest. She ran in an erratic pattern, calling Ethan's name. Sarah and Bryan moved slower. Desperate, Sarah searched the lower levels of the forest for a flash of orange or yellow.

Mackenzie ran deeper into the forest shouting Ethan's name. Her voice grew hoarse. She stopped when they were completely surrounded by trees and the house could no longer be seen. She lifted her head toward the forest canopy. "Ethan," she whispered. A tear trailed down her cheek.

Sarah placed her hand in Mackenzie's. She closed her eyes. Silence descended like a shroud.

Please, God, please.

"Hey," Bryan spoke in a soft hush.

Sarah opened her eyes and followed the direction of Bryan's pointing. From beneath thick evergreen boughs slanted close to the ground, two feet with one yellow and one orange sock were visible.

Mackenzie gulped air. "Ethan." She darted toward the tree and reached in through the branches, pulling out a blond child who pressed his face against her chest, not saying a word as Mackenzie laughed and cried. "Oh, thank You. Thank You, God."

After both mother and child calmed down, Bryan approached them. "Will he talk to us? He might know something about the men who took April."

Ethan grunted in protest and gripped the neck of his mother's shirt. Mackenzie made a soothing noise and stroked the little boy's head. "He might give you yes and no answers."

"Ethan, did you see the men who took your sister?"

No response.

Mackenzie repeated the question. Ethan nodded.

"Did you follow them?"

Again, Mackenzie had to repeat the question before Ethan responded in the affirmative.

"Which way did they go?"

With his face still pressed against his mother's chest, Ethan pulled his arm away from his body and pointed through the forest.

Bryan's gaze cut through the trees as he nodded slowly. "So they did take the old logging road." He turned to face Mackenzie. "We're going to get your daughter back." Bryan raced to the house. Several other police cars and a search-and-rescue unit with tracking dogs had arrived.

Bryan explained where he thought Mason and his men had gone and pointed out Mackenzie as she emerged from the forest carrying Ethan. "I'm going to get the jump on this." He looked over at Sarah. "You coming with me?"

He jogged toward the car, not giving Sarah time to respond. She raced after him. Once inside the car, he explained his urgency. "It'll take them twenty minutes to get this search organized and to get the dogs onto some kind of scent." He shifted gears. "That's twenty minutes we don't have."

Mackenzie ran toward them holding a canvas tote. Sarah rolled down her window.

"This is April's baby bag. If…when you find her, she'll be hungry and scared. She'll need these things."

"Thank you." Sarah draped her hand over the other woman's. "We're going to find her."

Mackenzie stepped away from the car.

Bryan sped up the road until he came to a spur road that must be the logging road Mackenzie had referenced.

"Why would they go this way? It'll take them forever to get back into town," Sarah said.

"I doubt their plan is to go into town just yet. They don't want to be caught. Mason's got Nadia suitably frightened."

"You really think he will just give up the baby so he can have Nadia?"

"Yes, I think April is a tool to him. But I have a feeling he won't be satisfied with just having Nadia back as his girlfriend. He's probably figured out we've been prepping her to testify. He's knows I'm back on the case. I think if Nadia goes back to him, she'll disappear...forever."

Judging from the frightened look on Sarah's face, Bryan feared he had said too much. He softened his tone. "Mason's only objective in life is to survive and to keep on doing whatever benefits him."

Sarah shook her head in stunned disbelief. "Certainly, he doesn't think he can stay in Discovery conducting business as usual."

"He'll probably tie up loose ends, disappear and reinvent himself in another part of the world." Bryan pounded the steering wheel as determination coursed through him. "We have to get this guy."

The car lumbered up the steep road and Bryan shifted down. He hoped his gamble would pay off. Trusting the testimony of a frightened four-year-old boy, who perceived the world differently than most, might not have come out of the police rulebook, but he had a gut feeling.

They'd lost precious time. He had to find a way to make up for it. The car laboriously climbed the hill. Once they reached the peak, Bryan turned the engine off. "Let's see if we can spot anything."

The mountain was a high point that provided a three-sixty-degree view of the surrounding area. The only higher spot was about two miles away as the crow flies, the mountaintop where the fire spotter tower stood. This part of the hill had very little vegetation. Thick forest occupied the lower elevations with barren areas that had been logged.

Bryan pulled the binoculars out of his glove box. "If they came this way, they took that road down there." He put the binoculars up to his eyes. The thick forest limited his view of the winding road. He turned in the opposite direction. Though the house wasn't visible from this angle, he spied the police and search-and-rescue vehicles moving out from a central point.

Sarah stared off in the distance at a plume of smoke rising up from the forest. Her hand fluttered to her mouth.

"That's a long ways away and it's a small area," he said.

"They wouldn't call off the search because of a fire, would they?" Anxiety laced through her words.

"That fire is miles from where these guys have probably gone," Bryan tried to assure her even as doubt crept in.

The fear in her eyes intensified.

Bryan studied the distant fire again. "Something that small will be contained quickly."

He examined the ant trails of dirt roads that crisscrossed through the hills, disappearing in patches of forest and emerging on the other side.

"There." Sarah pointed to the adjoining hill. Metal reflected the sunlight. A blue vehicle made its way down the mountain. "It's got to be them."

He assessed the direction the other police vehicles had gone. None of them headed the right way.

A revelation sparked in his mind. "That day Mason's men brought you out here, why did they take you all the way out here into the backcountry?"

"They intended to kill me." Sarah shuddered. "They probably thought no one would find the body out here."

"That's probably why they didn't kill you right away in town or me when they had me. The best way for Mason to stay clean is for the bodies never to be found." That had to have been what happened to Eva.

"Why are you being so morbid?"

"I'm not. What I'm asking is did you get the impression that either of those men who took you knew this area? People usually don't choose new and strange places like that for committing a crime."

Sarah seemed perplexed by the questions. "My eyes were covered for most of the journey."

He could tell by the tightness of her mouth and furled eyebrows that she really didn't want to relive any part of that day. He spoke gently. "Try to remember what they said. It's important."

She thought for a moment. "One of them did seem to know the area. He barked directions at the other man who was driving."

"So my bet is that same thug is with Mason now, guiding him through all these back roads so he's not likely to get caught. They're not going to take the obvious route. They want to avoid detection. And at least one of them knows where he's going."

They got back in the car and went down the other side of the mountain, entering a stretch of road that had thick forest on either side. The light diminished by half. They came to a place where the road forked in two directions. Bryan gave his best guess which way to turn based on the direction the other vehicle had been traveling. The road narrowed and turned into a washboard.

Though he kept his doubts to himself, he wondered if they had made the right choice. That vehicle they saw could have belonged to anyone.

The forest thinned. A helicopter flew overhead.

"Is that headed toward the fire we saw?"

Bryan peered up through the windshield. "Yeah, it might be."

The whop-whop-whop-whop of helicopter blades faded. Bryan made slow progress on the precarious road. He traveled at less than fifteen miles an hour as they rounded a bend. A creek flowed in front of them…

…and a blue truck just like the one they'd seen at a distance sat motionless in the middle of the creek.

Bryan tapped his hands on the steering wheel. "Looks like they tried to ford the creek and got stuck."

Judging from the amount of mud on the vehicle, they'd put substantial effort into trying to get it out. Sarah leaned her head out the window, listening. Only the creaking of the trees and a distant caw of a bird pressed on her ears. "I don't think they're close."

"Let's check it out, make sure the truck was really them." Bryan pressed on the handle and quietly eased the door open.

Sarah remained on high alert as she followed behind Bryan. The pounding of her feet on the dirt seemed exaggerated. The cool water swirled around her ankles as she stepped into the creek. The license plate was for Discovery's county and the frame around the plate was from Crazy Ray's, a tenuous connection. The tinted windows didn't allow her to see anything inside. At the center of the creek, where the vehicle bogged down, the water rose up past her knees. Her shoes sank into the mud. Sarah opened the passenger-side door. A toddler-sized windbreaker lay on the seat.

Bryan opened the driver's-side door. Sarah pointed to the windbreaker and he nodded.

"Check the registration," Bryan whispered.

She opened the glove compartment. The car was registered to a Richard Hart. She shrugged her shoulders, indicating that the information wasn't helpful. They both closed the doors at the same time.

Bryan met her at the front of the car. "I say we go up this road a ways. The windbreaker is enough for me to think it might be April."

They pushed through the muddy water and out onto the road. They'd gone only a hundred yards when the faint cry of a child reached their ears. Sarah's heart ached for the little girl. Bryan pointed in the direction the sound had come from and made a motion indicating they should separate and surround the area.

Sarah crept through the brush. The crying stopped. She heard men's muffled voices and then the crying started up again. Her foot snapped a twig. She cringed, but there was no interruption in the men's conversation. The voices grew louder, more distinct as she got closer. She crouched low and peered out from beneath the brush. There were two men, both of them armed with handguns. A rifle sat propped up against a rock. She recognized one of the men as Acne Scars, one of her kidnappers.

April stood at the center of the clearing. No one held her, no one comforted her. Her voice had grown hoarse from crying. She swiped at her eyes and plumped down in the dirt. A man she recognized from Bryan's files as Tyler Mason stood some distance away from the other men, talking on the phone. The conversation indicated that he was making arrangements for someone to come and get them. Mason hung up the phone and paced.

April, a little wobbly on her feet, dumped down to a crawling position and veered away from the two men.

"Get her," Mason commanded, still holding the phone to his ear.

One of the thugs grabbed April above the elbow and dragged her toward him. April shook her head several times and let out a sputtering sob.

Sarah peered across the clearing, hoping to see Bryan.

How were they going to rescue that little girl? They were outmanned and had only one gun.

Mason dialed another telephone number. "Hello, is this Discovery Police Station? I have a message for you to pass on to Nadia Akulov. Tell her she has five hours to meet at the rendezvous point. She'll know what I'm talking about. If she doesn't show or she brings police with her, no one will ever see April again. Can you manage that?"

Despite the midday heat, a chill coursed through Sarah's bones. A hand touched her back. She jumped but managed to stifle a scream. Bryan took her hand and pulled her deeper into the woods. He leaned close and whispered in her ear. "Go to the car, get it turned around and wait." He pressed the car keys into her hand. "It may be ten minutes, it may be an hour. Wait for me and be ready to go."

The plan seemed foolhardy at best, but she nodded. Right now, all they had was foolhardy. Sarah ran quietly but quickly back to the car. It took some maneuvering to get it turned around on the narrow road. Perspiring from her effort, she shifted the car into Park. Her pulse drummed in her ears as she watched the rearview mirror.

TWENTY-ONE

Bryan crept in close to the clearing. He watched. He waited. What he needed was an opportunity. Just a few seconds when all three of the men dropped their guard. None of them seemed to want to hold April, which was good. Mason strode away from the group, his back to the others as he talked on the phone to whoever was supposed to come and get them. This time his words were harsher, filled with anger and impatience.

One of the men rose from the flat rock where he'd been sitting. "I got to go water a tree."

April sat on the ground. Her head bobbed as she nodded off. Now all he needed was for the other man to be distracted. He picked up a rock and threw it so it hit a tree some distance away. The second hired gun ran toward the sound, leaving April unattended.

He wasn't going to get a better chance than this. He scrambled into the clearing, grabbed April and put his hand over her mouth to keep her from making a sound before slipping back into the thick brush.

The disrupting cries from the men pressed in on him.

Bryan clutched the child and slipped deeper into the forest. "I'm not going to hurt you, baby girl," he said in the most soothing voice he could manage while he tried to figure out what to do. He couldn't run right out to the road. They'd find him.

He hid behind a rock, gathering April close to his chest. She gazed up at him. Soft lashes framed her dark brown eyes. She clutched his shirt at the collar. She studied him, but did not cry out. His heart melted over her vulnerability.

One of the men ran by the rock. He could hear the other crashing through the trees, getting farther away. Mason screamed and cursed, every word filled with rage. Bryan peered out from behind the rock. No movement, no close sound. Now was the moment. Holding April tight, he sprinted from tree to tree to shield himself from view.

He worked his way back toward the creek, while the men shouted all around him. April clung to his collar. He held her close. Finally, the creek and the car came into view. Moving in spurts, he darted from a tree to a rock.

The men's voices grew louder behind him. He'd be fully exposed once he crossed the creek. He ran through the water, frustrated with the way the mud slowed him. Sarah had left the passenger-side door open, but would he get there in time? A rifle shot sounded behind him. April pressed harder against him.

Sarah started the car rolling even before he slid into the passenger seat. He leaned out, grabbed the door and slammed it shut as she sped up. April trembled against him.

He touched her silky hair. "It's all right." He circled his arms around her. She tilted her head and gazed at him. "You didn't make a peep, did you?"

She stuck a finger in her mouth. The thugs got off several rounds before Sarah slipped behind a bend. Each shot made April flinch. She looked at him, eyes filled with trust.

Sarah drove without slowing, checking behind her several times. Finally her grip on the wheel relaxed. She glanced over at Bryan and April. "She knows you won't hurt her. That's why she's so quiet."

Bryan chuckled. "Either that or she's so scared she's

speechless." His heart swelled with affection for this help-less creature.

"The bag Mackenzie gave us is on the floor by your feet."

Bryan leaned forward and picked up the baby tote. He opened it, pulling out a cup with a lid that was half-full of amber liquid.

April made a "ba" sound and reached for the sippy cup. Bryan pulled out a stuffed cat. "You want this?"

She looked at him and then at the toy. He tucked it close to her armpit and she held on to it. April took several gulps of juice from her cup.

"They probably didn't think to feed her or give her water." Sarah's voice was filled with indignation.

Sarah increased her speed as the road evened out and the car rolled over the hills. She looked down at her in-strument panel. "The gas gauge is going down really fast. They might have hit our tank when they shot at us."

"I think we might have bigger problems than that." Bryan pointed up the road at the approaching car. "I think that's Mason's ride out of here."

Sarah sucked air through her teeth. "Maybe they'll slip past us and think we're just a family out enjoying the wil-derness."

Still about two hundred yards away, the car edged to-ward them.

Bryan glanced out his window. His mind raced with possibilities for escape. "This is Mason we're talking about. He probably phoned ahead and alerted them about us."

"What do we do?" Sarah scanned the road, panic evi-dent in her voice.

Bryan slumped down in his car seat and angled April so she was lying down and not visible through the win-dow. "The road veers off up here. Hurry. See if you can get there before they pass us." Not much of a plan. For sure, the men had seen their car.

Sarah adjusted her hands on the steering wheel. "Are we hoping that Mason hasn't alerted them?"

"Yes, and we're hoping that these guys aren't even connected to Mason. We're hoping all sorts of unrealistic things."

Sarah pressed the accelerator. "The gas needle's on empty anyway. We're not going to get very far."

The car was within fifty yards of them. He couldn't see the driver or the passenger clearly. Sarah turned her head so the driver wouldn't have a clear view of her, either. She veered off on the spur Bryan had pointed out. The car eased past them just as their car lumbered up the side road.

Bryan craned his neck. "Can't see them anymore. Maybe we're safe."

"Should I try to get back on that road?"

Bryan leaned over and looked at the instrument board. "We'll run out of gas before then. Take this thing as far as it will go. Then we'll hike up the road. If Mason got cell reception, I should be able to also. One of the other searchers has to be close." Bryan gazed down at April, who had fallen asleep in his arms.

Sarah glanced over at him, her expression warming. "She seems really comfortable with you."

"Yeah. Weird, huh?"

The car chugged. Sarah pumped the gas. "That's all she wrote."

"Let's get to the top of that hill." Still holding a sleeping April, Bryan pushed the door open. He rested the little girl against one shoulder and hoisted the baby bag onto the other. "Phone Grant Pittman." He recited a number to her. "He's part of the search."

Sarah pressed the numbers. She waited. "He's not picking up."

Bryan adjusted the sleeping child in his arms. "She's getting heavy."

"I saw a sling in the bag." Sarah rooted through the tote and pulled out what looked like a long piece of fabric. "We can take turns carrying her."

"I'll go first. Once we contact someone, we'll have to walk out to where they can find us." Bryan glanced down the hill. The men in the car must have decided picking up Mason was their priority—but once Mason was in the car, Bryan was sure he'd start tracking them. "Mason and his men will be looking for us soon."

"I know. We'd better hurry." She flung the sling over Bryan's shoulder and fastened it.

"Here, let me take her for a second." April stirred but didn't wake when Sarah gathered her into her arms.

Bryan held the sling open so Sarah could place the toddler in it. He cut a glance through the trees toward the road. "I still don't see them." He looked down at April as she slept. It was his responsibility to get the three of them out of here unharmed.

"At least they won't be able to bring their car where we're going. We've got a head start on them." Sarah held up the phone. "Who do you want me to call now?

"Try Jake."

"Jake? The guy who picked us up when the men brought me to the lake?"

Bryan nodded and recited a number to her. "He lives close. He'll be able to get here fast."

They hiked the remaining distance to the ridge. Bryan continued to glance over his shoulder. He thought he saw the shimmer of a car through the trees, but couldn't be sure.

Sarah stood at the top of the ridge. Her spine went stiff.

"What's wrong?"

"I think we have more pressing issues than Mason."

Bryan walked up to where Sarah stood. He tensed at what he saw.

Patches of fire dotted the landscape below. Flames engulfed the mountain opposite them.

TWENTY-TWO

"Those fires are still pretty far away, right?" Even Sarah could hear that she sounded like she was trying to convince herself. Her gaze darted nervously toward him as fear took up residence in her knotted stomach.

"The problem is roads may be cut off. Help might not be able to get to us." Bryan's voice gave away no anxiety, though he must be in just as much turmoil as she was.

His calm fortified her own. "So how are we going to get out of here?"

Bryan resumed walking along the ridge, taking long strides. "We have to try to reach someone. Notify them of our position."

Sarah scrambled to keep up. "Okay, so give me a second and I'll keep trying to reach Jake."

"We don't have time to spare." Bryan walked even faster. April stirred in his arms. He patted her head, soothing her. "Maybe if we can get to an open area, a helicopter can reach us."

"We could try sneaking back down the road. We know the fires aren't in that direction."

"Too risky," Bryan said.

"So what are you saying?" Sarah spoke between breaths as she jogged beside Bryan.

He pointed toward the horizon. "We need to get to fire

tower six. There's a helicopter landing pad not too far from there. We can call for help on the radio. Someone might even still be there."

Sarah stared down at the forest below. Plumes of smoke rose up in at least three places.

Bryan stopped. He leaned close to her, their shoulders touching. He traced a path down the mountain and up the other side. "That's where we'll go. I think we'll be able to avoid the worst part of the fires."

Sarah looked down the mountain in the direction they'd come. A man in a light-colored shirt moved along the tree line. He held a rifle. "Let's get down on the other side of this mountain."

They hiked across the barren part of the mountain into the forest. When Sarah glanced up at the ridgeline, three men stood watching the forest below. She picked up her pace. Despite having to carry April, Bryan stayed ahead of her.

Several deer ran by them and the faint smell of smoke lingered. They walked for at least twenty minutes before Bryan suddenly stopped. He tilted his head toward the sky. "I need to get my bearings. See where that tower is at. Hold her for a minute."

Sarah lifted April out of the sling, which woke her. Thankfully, she didn't seem to mind shifting over to Sarah. The baby nestled against her, her forehead glistening with sweat. Despite the tree canopy, the forest seemed to be getting hotter.

Bryan walked over to an evergreen with low branches and proceeded to climb it. Sarah rooted through the baby bag and found a package of crackers for April. With April settled chewing on her food, Sarah dialed Jake's phone number.

"Hello?"

"Jake. This is Sarah Langston. I'm the one who—I'm a friend of Bryan Keyes." Sarah explained their situation.

Jake said, "Bryan was right about road access. They're not letting anybody into that area at this point."

"We're going to try to make it to fire tower six." Sarah pressed the phone against her ear. "That's the closest place where a chopper might be able to land."

"I'll do everything I can to alert the authorities that you're trapped in there. I can let the police department know, too."

"Thanks, I'll try to stay in phone contact."

Sarah hung up the phone. April offered her a bite of her half-chewed cracker. Sarah touched the little girl's soft cheek. "Thanks, sweetie."

Bryan shouted from the tree. "I think I see our route."

The sound of branches breaking alerted Sarah to someone or something moving through the forest. She gathered April more tightly in her arms and slipped behind a tree. Any hope that it was some animal fleeing the fire faded when she heard human voices. Sarah peered out from behind the tree. Her breath caught. She'd left the brightly colored baby bag out in the open.

Mason's men moved through the forest, their voices growing louder. Sarah gazed up and over at Bryan, who had concealed himself in the thick boughs.

Sarah remained still. April made a "ba ba ba" sound and kicked her leg. Sarah placed her fingers gently over April's mouth, hoping she'd understand.

The men's voices quieted.

April pulled Sarah's hand away and shook her head.

Sarah squeezed her eyes shut.

Please, don't make any noise.

She heard what could have been a footstep. And then another. Her heart pounded in her rib cage. Sweat trickled past her temple. April played with her necklace, touched her earrings. Several minutes passed.

Bryan poked his head through the branches. "I think they went past."

"Was it them?"

He climbed out to the end of a thick branch and dropped down. "I heard them, but never saw them, so I can't be sure."

"What if they're out in front of us now?"

April held her hands up to Bryan. He gathered her into his arms. "That's a chance we're going to have to take. We're not that far from the tower."

Her sense of direction had gotten completely turned around. "Will we be going by the lake?"

"No, we'll come in on the other side. No high, steep mountain to climb." He started walking with April looking back over his shoulder. Sarah walked behind. April waved at her. At least the little girl had no idea what kind of danger she was in.

Before long, they hit a wall of heat. In the distance, she could hear trees crashing to the ground. The air filled with smoke. April coughed.

Bryan tore off a piece of his shirt. "Is there water in that bag?"

Sarah dropped the bag on the ground and rooted through it. "There's a juice box."

Bryan saturated the piece of cloth with the liquid and then tore off two more pieces of fabric and wet them down, as well. "Put this over your mouth. Help me get April back in the sling."

All of them were sweating. The temperature had to be past a hundred. The air grew thicker and hazier with smoke. Bryan increased his pace. The trees thinned, and they stepped into a clearing.

Bryan pointed off in the distance. The dome-shaped roof of the tower rose above a rock formation.

Almost there.

Bryan raced up the tower stairs. By the time Sarah had entered the tower, he had set April on the floor. He ran around the tower closing all the windows.

Sarah glanced around. "Where's the fire spotter?"

"He must have left once he saw the fire down below. Fire should move downhill toward the lake. Smoke inhalation is our biggest worry," he said.

April picked up a cup and tried to drink. Sarah found bottled water and poured some into April's sippy cup.

Bryan picked up the radio. "This is fire tower six. I have an emergency situation here."

Dispatch came on the line. "Fire tower six was evacuated twenty minutes ago."

The smoke outside grew thicker.

"This is Bryan Keyes." Sweat trickled down his face. "I manned this tower up until a few days ago. I'm here with a woman and the missing nine-month-old child. Can you send in a chopper to get us?"

"Let me see what I can do. Out," said the dispatcher. She came back on the line minutes later. "Fire tower six. We have a bird that is approximately seven minutes away. Can you get to the landing pad by then?"

"We'll be there." Bryan clicked off the radio. His eyes darted around the room. He grabbed a blanket and one of the water bottles. "Wet this down. Your clothes, too."

They worked frantically and were out the door and down the stairs in less than three minutes. Bryan wrapped the damp blanket around April and held her close to his chest. The mechanical noise of the chopper grew louder as they ran. They zigzagged around a burning tree. April cried. Bryan held her tighter. Sarah grabbed hold of his shirt as the smoke thickened.

The helicopter sounded like it was on top of them though it was still some distance away. Smoke obscured their view. Sarah coughed. Finally the helicopter descended, creating an intense wind. April coughed and cried.

Bryan signaled Sarah to get into the helicopter first. He handed April to her and then climbed in himself.

The helicopter lifted off. Sarah belted into a seat, holding on tight to April. Bryan leaned forward and spoke to the pilot. "There are at least four other men stranded out there."

Whatever Mason and his men had done, they didn't deserve to die in this fire—no one did.

"Roger that, we can send another chopper to search the area," said the pilot.

As the helicopter gained elevation, Bryan stared out the window at the landscape below. The fire had jumped in some areas, creating patches of forest that were black or burning while others were untouched.

The pilot radioed ahead. The helicopter set down not too far from Mackenzie and Christopher's home. Mother and father stood outside their house along with little Ethan, but all three of them ran toward the chopper as it came down. Bryan climbed out first. Sarah handed over April.

The parents tearfully gathered April in their arms, thanking and hugging both Sarah and Bryan. They walked back to the house, mother holding baby, father carrying Ethan on his hip with his arm around mother. A happy family. Nadia emerged from the house and ran toward the family.

"What's that about?" Bryan grabbed Sarah's hand.

"I imagine Nadia just wanted to see that April was okay."

Two police officers stood behind the family, watching their surroundings and Nadia.

The family embraced Nadia.

"She gets to see April even after the adoption?"

"Limited contact. But Chris and Mackenzie agreed to send Nadia pictures and a letter every now and then letting her know how April is doing." She turned to face him. "It's the way I set up the adoption with Marie. You had already stopped speaking to me by then, once you signed away parental rights. I made those decisions on my own."

The pain in her voice stabbed at his heart. Bryan's throat tightened. He hadn't let himself think of these things for ten years. "You have pictures of Marie?"

Sarah nodded. "She was adopted by a couple in Wyoming. I got to meet them."

Bryan leaned close, kissing Sarah on the cheek. "I'm sorry I did that to you, left you like that."

Sarah turned toward him. Her eyes filled with love. "You're forgiven."

Warmth pooled around Bryan's heart. The sincerity of her words made him feel as though he'd been released from the cage he'd been in for ten years.

Grant approached them. "Could you two use a ride back into town?"

Bryan nodded. Grant led them to his patrol car. Bryan and Sarah sat together in the backseat holding hands, but not speaking.

As they came to the outskirts of town, Grant spoke. "Chief wants to debrief you about what happened out there with Mason. He's got kidnapping charges against him now. That guy is going away for a long time.

If he gets out of the forest alive.

"Sarah, I think he's going to want a statement from you, too," added Grant.

They entered the quiet station. Sarah gave her statement and then wandered out into the break room where she settled on the couch that had become her home away from home. After he completed his statement, Bryan found her asleep there. He shook her shoulder.

"Hey, I borrowed a friend's car. I can take you home."

Sarah sat up, joy evident in her voice. "I can go home?"

"They managed to rescue one of Mason's men out of the forest. It looks like the others perished—Mason included."

Sarah let out a breath. "So there won't be a trial."

Bryan shook his head. "Nadia is staying one night at the hotel. It's all set up for her, and she doesn't have anywhere else to go."

"Can we swing by the hospital to see how Crew is doing?"

"Sure," Bryan said.

Bryan drove through town and found a parking spot close to the hospital entrance. Still holding hands, they entered the hospital. The woman at the nurses' station stood up when she saw them coming.

"Hey." The nurse studied them from head to toe.

They must be quite a sight. She'd rinsed her face off at the police station, but looking over at Sarah, Bryan registered that her clothes were torn, dirty and smelled like smoke.

"Crew regained consciousness about an hour ago," said the nurse.

Sarah rushed toward his room and flung open the door. Bryan followed behind. Crew was sitting up in his hospital bed. He looked pale and weak, but a light came into his eyes when she entered the room. "Hey, little sister."

She wrapped her arms around him. "I thought I'd lost you."

Sarah's joy was infectious.

"Haven't seen you in a while." Crew offered Bryan a weak salute.

"Took me ten years to get back," Bryan said.

"Well, you were the best thing for my sister." Crew ruffled Sarah's hair.

Sarah blushed. "That was a long time ago."

They visited for a few minutes more until Crew started to nod off. Sarah kissed his forehead and walked out with Bryan.

They drove in silence. The street light flashed by and then thinned out.

"Do you think what Crew said is true, about you being a good thing for me?" She turned in her seat. Her gaze weighed on him.

"I think he had it backward. You were easy to be with, easy to love." He adjusted his hands on the steering wheel as the familiar stab of pain shot through him. "We were so young. We made mistakes."

She reached over, draping her hand on his. Her touch eased his hurt.

"We'll always have regrets. When I said you were forgiven, I meant it. Now you just have to forgive yourself."

Her words were a soothing balm soaking through him, melting the hurt and the self-hate he'd lived with for so many years. They had made some wrong decisions as a couple, but they'd made the right decision for their little girl. Were they ready now to move on from the past, and have the future they'd tried to rush before?

Bryan turned onto the gravel road that led to Sarah's house. The tires crinkled over the road when he slowed down.

"I'm sure your cat will be glad to see you." His attempt at joviality had a ring of sadness to it. What were they to each other now that all this was over? Mason was dead. He had no more excuse to be with her.

"Mr. Tiddlywinks is pretty independent. Though I'm sure he'll have some choice words for the neglect he's suffered." When Bryan pulled into the driveway, she turned to face him. "Walk me to the door? I have something I want to show you."

Sarah stepped inside and turned on a single light over her desk. She opened a drawer and pulled out a photograph, taking it to Bryan where he waited by the door.

"It's Marie. She was in a dance recital recently." She placed it in his hand and then wrapped her hand around his. "You can keep it. I have another copy."

A bright-eyed, smiling little girl stared back at him. He touched the picture with his finger. She had the same curly brown hair as Sarah, but the slightly crooked nose and round eyes were his. His throat tightened. He gazed up at Sarah.

He gathered her into his arms and kissed her. Her lips were warm and inviting. He rested his hand against her back and pulled her closer, deepening the kiss. He held her for a long moment, his forehead pressed against hers. He didn't want to go but his feelings jumbled up inside of him and he couldn't find the words. He pulled away from her, turned and walked toward the door.

Sarah stood stunned from the power of his kiss. Outside, she heard the car door slam and the engine roar to life. She turned on a kitchen light.

"Mr. Tiddlywinks. Here, kitty kitty." As she wandered through the house a pungent odor surrounded her. She couldn't quite place it.

She switched on the light in her bedroom, checking under the bed where Mr. Tiddlywinks liked to hide. No cat.

Sarah sniffed the air. Smoke. Did her clothes smell that bad? She took a hasty shower and put on fresh clothes, throwing the smelly ones in the outside garbage.

She returned to the living room. The acrid stench lingered. She opened several windows. Her cat was outside running his paws up and down the glass of the patio door.

Sarah's breath hitched. She'd left the cat inside the last time she was here. Her pulse skyrocketed. Now she knew why the smell of smoke was still so strong. Mason was in her house.

Sarah ran toward the front door as fast as she could.

Not fast enough.

TWENTY-THREE

Bryan made it to the end of the street. He pulled the car over and clicked on the dome light, staring down at the picture Sarah had given him. Bright eyes and a mass of curls. What a beautiful child. The hardness around his heart melted away.

He'd kissed Sarah wishing he could tell her he wanted to start over with a clean slate, but he couldn't manage to get the words out. Maybe tomorrow he'd give her a call when he wasn't so tongue-tied. He pulled out on the road that led back into town. Cars blipped by him. He was within a few blocks of his house when he realized his house wasn't where he wanted to be. Who was he kidding? This wasn't something that could wait another day. He loved her.

He scanned the road looking for a place to turn around. Hopefully, she hadn't already gone to bed.

Tyler Mason slammed Sarah's head against the wall. She slipped down to the floor.

"Where is she? Where's Nadia?"

Sarah's vision filled with dark spots as she turned around to face her attacker.

Mason grabbed her by her shirt, yanking upward and smashing her back against the wall. His face was close enough for her to feel his hot breath. "You'd better tell me now."

She shook her head. "She deserves a life, a chance to get away from you." Mason smelled so heavily of smoke, it made her nauseous. A streak of black marred his face. "How did you get out? They said you were dead."

He pushed her harder against the wall. "I have resources you couldn't begin to comprehend. What was one more helicopter flying around in the air?"

Mason's henchmen must have gotten separated. Mason had left the others to die.

His eyes bulged as he leaned close. "You'd better tell me in the next three minutes or it's curtains for you. And then for your brother. And then for your little boyfriend. And after I've disposed of all of you, I'll still find some other way to get to her."

Mason had lost everything. This wasn't about protecting his illegal business anymore. It was about revenge. He would kill Sarah either way. The least she could do was buy Nadia some time.

Mason grabbed her by the hair and dragged her into the kitchen. He pulled a kitchen knife out of the holder and then pushed her toward the back door.

"Open it," he said through clenched teeth.

She could hear the cat meowing as Mason pushed her down the stairs out into the field behind her house. She doubted he really cared all that much anymore about committing his crimes where no one would see them, but it had probably become such a habit that it didn't even occur to him to simply kill her inside, where her body would easily be found.

Bryan's face, the tenderness of his touch flashed in her mind. She loved him and now she would never see him again, never get to tell him how she felt.

Mason pushed her hard and she fell on her knees.

She closed her eyes. Her last thought was of Bryan and her prayer was that he would recover from losing her yet again.

* * *

When his knocking went unanswered, Bryan had let himself in. And from the moment he stepped across the threshold, he knew something was wrong. His gaze darted around and then he saw the open patio door. He rushed outside. Darkness covered the field.

Mason's voice, low and sinister, floated through the air. "Have it your way."

Bryan darted softly through the field, focusing on the direction Mason's voice had come from. He drew his weapon. He squinted. Was that a silhouette of a person, or a shadow? He lifted his gun and fired.

A scream filled the night air. Sarah's scream.

Bryan ran. Feet pounding. Heart racing. He gathered Sarah into his arms.

"He's dead," she whispered, pressing close against his chest.

His arms enveloped her.

"What made you come back? How did you know?"

He touched her soft hair. "I didn't know. I…wanted to tell you I love you."

She touched his cheek, kissed his lips and then pressed close against his chest. His heart pounded; heat radiated and adrenaline coursed through him. He closed his eyes, nestling his cheek against her head.

"I love you, too," she whispered. "I don't think I ever stopped loving you."

EPILOGUE

Through the window of the bridal shop, Sarah spotted Bryan standing out on the sidewalk. She felt a rush of joy as she stepped out to meet him.

He gathered her in his arms.

"You didn't see me when I came out in that last wedding dress, did you?"

Bryan raised his hand. "Scout's honor. I just got here from the station." He hooked his arm through hers as they walked past the downtown shops. "I have some good news. The last of Mason's henchmen have been taken into custody."

Sarah took in a breath of crisp September air. "That makes me feel a lot safer."

Bryan stopped at a storefront that read Jefferson Expeditions. "I read something about this guy. He takes people out in the wilderness and teaches them survival skills."

Sarah shrugged. "What does that have to do with anything?"

"I was thinking maybe we could do that for our honeymoon. You know, go tromping around the woods."

She caught the twinkle in his eye and gave him a friendly punch in the shoulder. "I think we've done enough of that."

Bryan slipped his hand into hers. They walked several more blocks to the café where they planned on eating. Bryan held the door for her and they found a quiet booth. Sarah rested her arms on the table and leaned toward Bryan. "I told you Crew said he'd give me away at the wedding, right?"

Bryan nodded.

"It seems he's bringing a date to the wedding." Sarah was buoyant with excitement.

The waitress arrived and set their menus in front of them.

"Oh, really, who is he bringing?"

"Me," said the waitress. Bryan registered surprise when he saw that their waitress was Nadia.

She had a warm glow to her cheeks and she had gained weight.

"You," said Bryan, shaking his head.

Nadia raised her head and squared her shoulders. "I give you folks few minutes think about what you want for your meals."

As Nadia walked away, Bryan continued to shake his head. "Some things come full circle, don't they?"

Feeling a surge of love for the man she wanted to spend her life with, Sarah grabbed Bryan's strong hands. "Yes, they do. And sometimes you get a second chance with your first love."

He squeezed her hand, love shining in his eyes. "Yes, indeed."

* * * * *

Dear Reader,

While this book is a fun and sometimes harrowing suspense story, I think it is also a book about choices and consequences. As teenagers Sarah and Bryan made destructive choices that caused deep wounds for both of them. Crew made choices that led him down a path to addiction, as well. Though we meet Tyler Mason when vengeance and control rule his soul, he, too, had to have made choices that turned him into a man without a conscience. When I thought about the spiritual journey of these characters, I wanted to show that our past choices don't have to determine who we become in the future. There is redemption for Bryan, Sarah and Crew because they decide to pursue what is good and right and true.

Some people might have looked at Sarah and Crew, unloved orphans lost in the foster care system, and said that there was no chance for them to have a normal life. Life circumstances can be truly terrible and filled with pain, but we still have choices to make. When my husband and I married, more than twenty-five years ago, I'm sure some people thought we wouldn't last a year. To look at our backgrounds, where we came from, that might have been a good prediction. He was the child of a terribly destructive divorce and I was the daughter of an alcoholic father. But then, we had choices to make, day by day, moment by moment.

Your redemption story may look different from Sarah and Bryan's. Not everyone gets a second chance at love with their teenage sweetheart. But everyone has the chance to find healing through the choices we make every day.

Sharon Dunn

Questions for Discussion

1. Have you ever become disillusioned about your career or life mission like Bryan does? What happened?

2. Bryan decides to spend time alone in the fire tower because he can no longer deal with the injustice he sees with his job. Do you think he made a good choice?

3. What did you think of Sarah's relationship with her brother, Crew? Why does she still love him?

4. Sarah's background as a foster care kid causes her to be treated with prejudice by Bryan's parents. How does Sarah overcome her childhood?

5. Have you ever known someone like Crew, a person who had goodness in them but made destructive choices?

6. What different choices could Sarah and Bryan have made when they were teenagers?

7. What forces pulled Bryan and Sarah apart when they were so young?

8. What was the most exciting scene in the book?

9. What was the most emotional scene in the book?

10. Have you ever known anyone who got a second chance at love like Bryan and Sarah do?

11. In what ways does Tyler Mason control and destroy Nadia's life?

12. What does Nadia do to get free of Tyler, both emotionally and physically?

13. Why do both Sarah and Nadia give up their daughters for adoption? Do you think they made the right choice?

14. Have you known anyone who gave up a child for adoption? What was the fallout from that choice? Did that person find a measure of healing and assurance in the aftermath?

15. Do you know someone who adopted a child? How was that person's life changed? What about the child?

REQUEST YOUR FREE BOOKS!
2 FREE RIVETING INSPIRATIONAL NOVELS
PLUS 2 FREE MYSTERY GIFTS

YES! Please send me 2 FREE Love Inspired® Suspense novels and my 2 FREE mystery gifts (gifts are worth about $10). After receiving them, if I don't wish to receive any more books, I can return the shipping statement marked "cancel." If I don't cancel, I will receive 4 brand-new novels every month and be billed just $4.74 per book in the U.S. or $5.24 per book in Canada. That's a savings of at least 21% off the cover price. It's quite a bargain! Shipping and handling is just 50¢ per book in the U.S. and 75¢ per book in Canada.* I understand that accepting the 2 free books and gifts places me under no obligation to buy anything. I can always return a shipment and cancel at any time. Even if I never buy another book, the two free books and gifts are mine to keep forever.

123/323 IDN F5AC

Name	(PLEASE PRINT)

Address	Apt. #

City	State/Prov.	Zip/Postal Code

Signature (if under 18, a parent or guardian must sign)

Mail to the Harlequin® Reader Service:
IN U.S.A.: P.O. Box 1867, Buffalo, NY 14240-1867
IN CANADA: P.O. Box 609, Fort Erie, Ontario L2A 5X3

**Are you a current subscriber to Love Inspired Suspense books
and want to receive the larger-print edition?
Call 1-800-873-8635 or visit www.ReaderService.com.**

* Terms and prices subject to change without notice. Prices do not include applicable taxes. Sales tax applicable in N.Y. Canadian residents will be charged applicable taxes. Offer not valid in Quebec. This offer is limited to one order per household. Not valid for current subscribers to Love Inspired Suspense books. All orders subject to credit approval. Credit or debit balances in a customer's account(s) may be offset by any other outstanding balance owed by or to the customer. Please allow 4 to 6 weeks for delivery. Offer available while quantities last.

Your Privacy—The Harlequin® Reader Service is committed to protecting your privacy. Our Privacy Policy is available online at www.ReaderService.com or upon request from the Harlequin Reader Service.
We make a portion of our mailing list available to reputable third parties that offer products we believe may interest you. If you prefer that we not exchange your name with third parties, or if you wish to clarify or modify your communication preferences, please visit us at www.ReaderService.com/consumerschoice or write to us at Harlequin Reader Service Preference Service, P.O. Box 9062, Buffalo, NY 14269. Include your complete name and address.

LIS13R

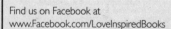

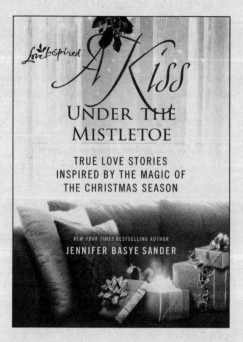

Christmas has a way of reminding us of what really matters—and what could be more important than our loved ones? From husbands and wives to boyfriends and girlfriends to long-lost loves, the real-life romances in this book are surrounded by the joy and blessings of the Christmas season.

Featuring stories by favorite Love Inspired authors, this collection will warm your heart and soothe your soul through the long winter. *A Kiss Under the Mistletoe* beautifully celebrates the way love and faith can transform a cold day in December into the most magical day of the year.

On sale now!

SPECIAL EXCERPT FROM

Love Inspired

Bygones's intrepid reporter is on the trail of the town's mysterious benefactor. Will she succeed in her mission?

Read on for a preview of
COZY CHRISTMAS
by Valerie Hansen, the conclusion to
THE HEART OF MAIN STREET *series.*

Whitney Leigh rolled her eyes. "Romance! It's getting to be an epidemic."

Because she was alone in the car, she didn't try to temper her frustration. Fortunately, this time, the editor of the *Bygones Gazette* had assigned her to write a new series about the Save Our Streets project's six-month anniversary. If he had asked her for one more fluff piece on recent engagements, she would have screamed.

Parking in front of the Cozy Cup Café, she shivered and slid out.

As a lifelong citizen of Bygones, she was supposed to have been perfect for the job of ferreting out the hidden facts concerning the town's windfall. Too bad she had failed. Instead of an exposé, she'd ended up filling her column with news of people's love lives. But she was not going to quit investigating. No, sir. Not until she'd uncovered the real facts. Especially the name of their secret benefactor.

She stepped inside the Cozy Cup.

"What can I do for you?" Josh Smith asked.

Whitney was tempted to launch right into her real reason for being there. Instead, she merely said, "Fix me something warm?"

"Like what?"

"Surprise me."

She settled herself at one of the tables. There was something unique about this place. And, truth to tell, the same went for the other new businesses on Main. Each one had filled a need and become an integral part of Bygones in a mere five or six months.

Josh Smith was a prime example. He was what she considered young, yet he had quickly won over the older generations as well as the younger ones.

He stepped out from behind the counter with a steaming cup in one hand and a taller, whipped-cream-topped tumbler in the other.

"Your choice," he said pleasantly, placing both drinks on the table and joining her as if he already knew this was not a social call.

"I see you're not too busy this afternoon. Do you have time to talk?"

"I always have time for my favorite reporter," he said.

"How many reporters do you know?"

"Hmm, let's see." A widening grin made his eyes sparkle. "One."

Will Whitney get her story and find love in the process?

Pick up COZY CHRISTMAS to find out.
Available December 2013
wherever Love Inspired® Books are sold.

Love the Love Inspired book you just read?

Your opinion matters.

Review this book on your favorite book site, review site, blog or your own social media properties and share your opinion with other readers!

Be sure to connect with us at:
Harlequin.com/Newsletters
Twitter.com/LoveInspiredBks
Facebook.com/LoveInspiredBooks